Listening
to Mozart

The

John

Simmons

Short

Fiction

Award

University of

Iowa Press

Iowa City

*Charles
Wyatt*

*Listening
to Mozart*

University of Iowa Press, Iowa City 52242

Printed on acid-free paper

Library of Congress Cataloging-in-Publication Data

Wyatt, Charles, 1943–

Listening to Mozart / Charles Wyatt.

p.   cm.—(The John Simmons short fiction award)

ISBN 0-87745-524-4

1. Flute players—United States—Social life and customs—

Fiction.   2. Man-woman relationships—United States—

Fiction.   I. Title.   II. Series.

PS3573.Y19L5   1995

813'.54—dc20   95-4777

                                                         CIP

01   00   99   98   97   96   95   C   5   4   3   2   1

For Cindy

With special thanks to

Judith Grossman,

Joan Silber,

John Skoyles,

and the Hambidge Center

Contents

ACKNOWLEDGMENTS

Some of the stories in this collection appeared,
in slightly different form, in the following
publications: "Leopard-Skin Pill-Box Hat,"
the *Texas Review*; "The Bagpipe," *Mid-
American Review*; "Mrdangam," *Quarterly
West*; "Teaching," *Hanging Loose*; "Ghosts,"
the *South Carolina Review*; "Indonesia,"
winner of the 1993 Chris O'Malley Prize in
Fiction, the *Madison Review*.

Bach Suite

My mind wanders dangerously when I play the flute. My thoughts float, dart, appear and disappear in mysterious comet-like ellipses. I hardly own them. When I was a child, I would construct elaborate fantasies as I practiced, and wake from them with no recollection of the scales I had played. I would imagine famous musicians standing outside my window, listening as I practiced, deeply moved by the music I had discovered among the tiny spiders clinging to the corners of my room; and if I had been foolish enough to have the radio on while I learned the notes of some difficult piece, I would have the precise, play-by-play recall of a ball game every time I played that particular passage. Later when I had my first job in an opera orchestra, I was terrified of losing my place in the rests. Counting measures always put me into a trance of daydreaming, and I had to resort to counting on my fingers, something I still do today. When my mind slipped away, the fingers would continue to mark the measures, and sometimes I could recapture the number. It's an awful feeling, in an opera you don't know well, to have lost the count—waiting for your next entrance, usually a solo, wondering if you will recognize it, if the conductor will cue you beforehand, or if he will only glare wrathfully when it is too late. Before all this, when I was a child, I would fall asleep listening to music, and wake hearing music no man had written, and that would drain away from me far too quickly, like water from a leaping fish. I grieved its loss, and I sought out its source in every piece of music I learned. I never found it, but sometimes I felt near. And never so near as in the mystical constructions, the crystal-like structures of J. S. Bach. Now, so many years later, I know from experience that this is one mystery I was not destined to penetrate, that all I can expect is to perform these great works, and endure the wanderings of my mind. And what do I think of? Of anything.

When I am playing a solo, as I am tonight, I think of what I must do afterward, of bowing. Of whether I shake the conductor's hand first or the concertmaster's. Or I think of all the times I have played this piece, or, more likely yet, I think of the hours spent practicing, of waiting to perform it, of imagining its performance. Where does the music come from? I might as well be asleep, where perhaps I still hear those unearthly symphonies. One part of me minds the music; and that is not a conscious thing, rather a kind of falling, a slow falling, like a dive into green water with the surface almost out of sight. And the other part is wading in cattails with my rod held high, thick rubber boots over my knees, the smell of the mud just released in bubbles around me as I step and sink, and the sudden jar of the water moccasin striking my leg.

Now I am standing in the wings, next to rows of stacked iron weights and cables stretching up into darkness, holding my flute in the most elegant way I can imagine, the way I hold it when I walk before an audience, as if it might bite me. I have played this piece at least a half-dozen times before. Six different conductors, six different orchestras, good and bad. This is not the best of those orchestras. The Bach Suite No. 2 in B Minor is not a concerto, and although it is scored for flute and strings with a very prominent flute part, the flute part frequently doubles the first violins, and instead of being a soloist, the flutist becomes part of the color of the massed violin sound. Inexperienced reviewers often complain of not always being able to hear the flute in performances of the piece. There's simply nothing to complain about; sometimes the flute is just another one of the fiddles. But audible or not, you have all of the endurance problems of a concerto. The suite takes about twenty to twenty-five minutes to play as the clock moves; a good nap for a relaxed listener, but a lifetime for the performer on the stage.

OUVERTURE
(lentement, allegro [fugato], lentement)

This time, as is often the case, and in spite of my disclaimer, the piece is being treated as a flute concerto. Management has an inexpensive soloist, the orchestra's principal flutist, so they trot him out front and give the audience something to look at and applaud. The piece was programmed more than a year ago by a Bach specialist who was to appear as a guest conductor this season. Unfortunately, he had to cancel all his appearances due to failing health, and our own assistant conductor (who doesn't even seem to like Bach) will lead the orchestra. We are opening the concert with this piece and I am waiting for him to take a few more puffs from a palmed cigarette before we can walk on stage. The audience applauds from the darkness beyond the stage lights. A few chairs squeak as last-minute adjustments are made to give me room. And we begin. The stately opening of the French-style overture is in a slow, double-dotted rhythm. Always two quick notes rushing to the accented held note or trill. Some of the more serious students of Baroque performance style play this introduction moderately fast, and the quick notes give it a kind of unrestrained energy. I don't understand how they can know how fast these things were played more than two hundred years ago, but I feel instinctively that they are right. Our assistant conductor asked me how I would like to do it, and I sang him a lively tempo. "Fine," he said. So why is he doing it twice as slow? He must have heard it this way when he was a boy, when the popular style of playing Bach was lugubrious, elephantine. We're going to be here all night. But I am just a soldier in this movement, with only a few notes different from the violins. If I tried to move the tempo I would wear myself out, and be drowned by the strings. The time I tried to rescue a fat man from snakes on the bank, I had a very small rowboat, and it rode about half an inch above the water. Just as we pushed up to the bank on the other side, the water rushed in, and we sank. I can see that boat pulled half out of the water, half full itself, with little perch cutting around like sharks.

The subject of a fugue must have a certain shape, something which will stand out against endless waves of eighth notes. It must sound like a fugue, look like a fugue, smell like a fugue. First one voice, then, at intervals of time, three others following, this time from the top down. There are episodes when the flute is the only instrument playing, and, as always in Bach, there is never any place to breathe. Beyond where the cables disappear in darkness, there are catwalks where I would have loved to climb when I was a child, but now I pass the ladders every day without thinking of them. A certain shape, a syncopated space through which to view what came before, even before it comes. Of course, I am thinking of the ladders now, of climbing them, and of looking down, my palms and fingers tingling as I hold the railing. The subject of a fugue must fit a shape remembered, fall into a place to come. This opening overture is the longest of the seven movements of the suite by far, and in modern times the repeat, mercifully, is usually omitted. It is early spring and the pond is rough on top with scribbles of wind. The subject of a fugue must smell like a fugue. It is early spring and I am wading in fragrant mud along the shallow end, trying to free my line from a snag about ten feet out. Almost on top of it, I pull upward as hard as I can, and it begins to give. There are places where I have made double pencil checks on the music to remind me to fill my lungs completely. There are long solo passages with chromatic descending notes alternating with a common repeated note, giving the effect of two instruments playing. But the breath must be there. Enough breath. It is a skeleton. My heart stops and I let it sink back into the brown water. The breath must be like a cry. All the air in an instant, not a gasp, but a sudden inrushing. There is friction and denial in a gasp. This breath is faith itself. Then I pull again. Slowly. Worried down to the bone on top by snapping turtles and fish, but something slow and heavy beneath, partially preserved by the icy water. Tonight there will be no repeat, and we are nearing the second ending. Now a return to a shorter version of the slow double-dotted material, and we cadence. I have to play louder and hope there will be some flute color in the string sound. If anything the tempo has grown slower with all the effort of this conductor. He tries to lead with his arm and body rather than the end of the stick. The violins are losing sound on the sustained notes as they run out of bow. The flute, on the other hand, has more room to breathe and is probably easier to hear now, significantly louder than the strings in the long notes. The overall effect of this movement is a sandwich, double-dotted bread with a fugue in the middle.

RONDEAU
(allegro)

A two-part form in duple time with flute solos in the second part. Most of the solos in this piece happen when the orchestra drops out and the flute keeps on going. There is a kind of relentless, persistent quality in the fast movements of most Baroque music, especially in Bach, that makes you feel the music was snatched out of the air, and that its beginning and ending in a performance are mere accidents. Often I'm standing in mud watching the sky in water. The wind shows its shape in the wrinkled space of that flat field. Sometimes a red-winged blackbird will hover over me, barely out of reach, protesting my encroachment on its nest in the cattails. I could have slapped at it with my fishing rod and lost my balance. My feet could have caught in the cattails, heavy waders sinking in their roots. Water could have rushed in at the top, filling them. Now I'm discovering the boundaries of my space. I have just stepped on the base of the music stand of the first desk second violins. The theme of this rondeau has breathing room, so it's particularly invigorating to play. I suppose I was moving too much.

SARABANDE
(andante)

A slow dance movement with a canon between the top line and the base at the interval of a fifth. I remember the second time I played this piece. The conductor was extremely vague bringing in the lower voice. Chaos resulted, and after a few bars of searching and groping, as if in a deep fog, we had to stop and start the movement again. A slow dance with a canon, but simpler in the low voice, the voice that must hold up all above, like the bottom tier of a Roman bridge. I could have started at the snake and pitched away from it, catching my feet in the bubbling tangle. I was so furious and humiliated I refused to come to the front of the stage for a bow after the performance. That left me with a furious and humiliated conductor to deal with for several more concerts. I have learned better since. Only last week, a conductor who had inexplicably stopped conducting in a very delicate moment, with the resultant train wreck, explained himself by saying, "I thought you could read my mind." This time I said nothing.

When I was a child I kept two baby snapping turtles in a bowl and fed them raw bacon. I can see them pulling at a strand and pushing the rest away with a curiously graceful foot. I have seen a grown adult, big as a washtub, swimming under ice, thin strands of moss trailing from the scalloped edge of its carapace. I rarely add ornamentation to this movement, although it is part of the tradition. Bach, unlike most Baroque composers, wrote out most of his ornamentation, and his bare-bones melodies are handsome in themselves.

BOURRÉE I—BOURRÉE II
(allegro)

Another fast dance in duple time, if anything, livelier than the rondeau. The second bourrée is flute solo, and a return to the first makes the whole effect another sandwich. I try to show the concertmaster how I am playing the repeats of the second part solo much softer, in an echo effect, because he's not listening. I know him well. When he takes the tuning A from the oboe, he thinks he can tune his violin with his bow arm. Up and down goes the bow furiously, but does he touch the tuning pegs? I make my echo effects in lonely splendor. The second flutist in the opera orchestra had held my job before I came. And his father had been the principal flutist in the opera before him. He even played on his father's flute. It was wonderfully loud, but its paper-thin metal couldn't hold the pitch, so he was always sharp when the music moved him. He did not take his demotion kindly. During my first opera performance, he reached over and turned the page of my part while I was in the middle of a solo. It was the most malicious thing I have ever known anyone do in a musical performance. But I had memorized my part. It didn't make a difference.

POLONAISE   (AND DOUBLE)
(moderato e staccato)

This polonaise is a stately dance with quick grace notes, a not-too-distant cousin to the opening lentement, but with more syncopation. In the double, the tune is played in the continuo only (with the cello and harpsichord), and the flute plays a wonderful staccato obbligato over it. Wonderful if I don't screw up the breathing. Good old Johann Sebastian—he never let practical considerations stand in the way of a good musical idea. We usually make the breathing work by slowing up at the end of a phrase now and then. It's all carefully worked out. When I played this piece the first time at my graduation recital, the cellist didn't show up for the performance. His last-minute replacement played through every breathing pause. There was one harassed, agitated, and gasping flutist on the stage. Now, at least we all agree on the tempo. Evenings I would stand facing west, fishing into the reflection of the sky above the departed sun. I could still see my lure floating when everything was deep in shadow on the land. At that time of day the water would grow calm as glass, but would grow in life, the thinnest membrane between the lighted sky and its own hidden breathing. As the wind died down, dark swirls would appear, and little popping sounds surrounded me as the water creatures grew active. I would fish and draw in the last fine light like an endless breath. My low notes are coming out cleanly—they're the first thing to go when I get tired—the secret to playing these wide intervals is not to force, not to "brass," the low register, as my old teacher used to say in his broken English. I could have fallen through the ice in winter. I could have. Once, when I had a handlebar mustache, an end crept into my mouth while I was playing a long sequential passage in a Bach solo sonata. The sound got fuzzier and fuzzier. There was nothing I could do, because there were no rests, nothing but eighth notes as thick as cattails and the flute tone windy as a hovering blackbird. Now we're back to the top of the polonaise, making the flute solo a sandwich again. The grace notes must snap like a flag in a changing wind. And the last note does not taper, but ends with a slap at the silence to follow.

MENUET
(allegretto)

A simple minuet in three-four time. I'm almost home and I'm gathering myself for what is to come next, the movement that allows this suite to pretend to be a flute concerto. Two parts. Keep the flute sound over the violins as much as possible. I could have cried out in surprise and the water would have been like a knife at the back of my nose. I would have felt it cold and strangling, filling me. I would have struggled. I don't know how long. I would not have known. I've got a lot more space to stand in now. Violinists have been easing away from me for the past ten minutes. I move a lot. I suppose it's my reaction to playing such a soft instrument. If they can't hear me, they can see me. Now, the Badinerie.

BADINERIE
(allegro)

Like the wind, and hope you don't stub your toe. I like to ornament the repeats. It's almost impossible to squeeze in extra notes, but it's a great effect, like standing up on the back of a galloping horse. I wonder if I could see myself from the catwalk. The sound is there, filling the darkness. I pulled and it began to give, so I waded toward it. I pulled and it eased upward, the way a heavy tree limb would give way. And it was the last thing I was looking for, rising out of darkness. I had to wait to know what I saw. I had to wait to want to run and wait to tell myself to wait and look again. All inside the shell of a second, like these notes here. And now the end comes. The last note ending with an accent, and the silence, for a second, or some part of a second, or more, strikes us hard, a kind of waking. Applause sounds like rain. Another thing it sounds like—I once woke up startled, at my cousin's house, with a cat purring about an inch away from my ear. Shake hands with the conductor. Careful, he's dripping. (You don't have to slash and lunge to conduct Bach.) Shake hands with the concertmaster. Bow deeply to the black the noise is coming from. Now, briskly off the stage. I'll take a solo bow. I smell the cigarette smoke from the wing behind me. It's over, the music is lost again. It's never farther from me than now. Now one more time for the orchestra. My hands are shaking. I've dropped my fishing rod in the muddy water in front of me. I can reach in and feel for it. My hand will disappear and I will feel the cold chill, but I will see nothing. I can surely touch it with my foot, but I can see nothing. I'm backing out of the water. One boot has sunk too deeply in the mud. I could be falling. Out of the darkness. How long have those bubbles waited in the mud for this? For them, too, it must be like falling. I can almost hear it.

Half a
Flute

Philadelphia, 1966

Richter was famous, although he must be dead by now. It has been nearly thirty years since my friend Jerry took me to his shop for the first time. It was in a shabby block just off Market street—I think I could find it today, although I suppose there's a good chance it's no longer there—I can almost smell the musty exhalation the streets gave out in the morning, before the sun was high enough to warm the dust and grime of his practically unmarked doorway. That door opened to a dim flight of stairs which led up to an even darker landing where there was a door with faint lettering on the glass: "W. O. Richter: Clarinets, Oboes, Bassoons." Richter's shop consisted of two rooms off the landing. You entered through the showroom, which was always empty except for an occasional visitor who did not feel comfortable enough to enter the workroom. Behind glass-fronted counters displaying a few dispirited antique cocuswood clarinets and bassoons, the walls were covered with framed and autographed photographs of unsmiling men, many of them affecting enormous handlebar mustaches and full, side-whiskered beards. They held oboes, English horns, clarinets, and bassoons in their sepia-tinted hands, and they were famous once, although I had scarcely heard of any of them. Their inscriptions were of gratitude to the master, to Richter, who, while he allowed dust to gather on their photographs, must have taken infinitely better care of the tools of their trade. This was the man to whom the most famous orchestral woodwind players would travel across the country, or across oceans for that matter. They brought him their ailing children, or better still, brought the raw, new ones to be recreated, tuned and bored.

That very morning, I watched from the doorway of the showroom in horror the apparently routine procedure of reaming at least a quart of beautifully curled shavings from the inside of a new clarinet, while Jerry silently beckoned me to come inside. Jerry, an oboist from Philadelphia, had promised to introduce me to Richter. There were several impatient, important-looking, but rather subdued men in the shop.

"Do you know who those guys are?" Jerry whispered. I didn't quite catch what followed, but it was CSO or BSO or something which I was sure stood for an illustrious visiting orchestra.

I wandered around, looking at the pictures, turning sideways at narrow corners between the wall and a large table stacked with instrument cases, and getting in the way all the same. There were a few more pictures in the workroom, but only one in color that I can remember, of an elderly man playing a flute with a parakeet perched on his shoulder. You could read the music on his stand, a Bach sonata. He was obviously an amateur, playing an antique wooden flute in a modern photograph, and the picture seemed out of place, but perhaps it indicated there was hope and tolerance for lesser lights and students like myself. My own teacher was in several of the photographs, with his stunning mane of white hair and stern expression. Yellowed programs of the New York Flute Club were impaled on a nail next to the door, and I read them curiously, wondering why they were there. The most recent one was ten years old. There was a filthy toilet in a little room in the corner, and the workroom, which was connected to the showroom by a short hallway, was under a skylight and had a sweeping view of rooftops and ailanthus trees. The skylight leaked, and foot-long strips of failing paint depended from the ceiling around it like Spanish moss. Everything was dated, falling apart, and in shades of gray and brown. The workbench, which extended along two walls, was a graveyard of old oboes, bassoon bocals, keyless flutes, reaming tools, screwdrivers, and other less identifiable objects. The overall impression was one of chaos and clutter with scarcely a square inch of free space.

When the important men left, Jerry brought me up to the bench where Richter was working.

"Mr. Richter, I'd like you to meet James Baxter, a classmate of mine."

"And what instrument do you play?" asked Richter, turning to gaze at me over his glasses, which had slipped precariously to the tip of his nose.

"I'm a flutist," I said, pleased that my voice didn't crack.

"He's fantastic," offered Jerry, who had a tendency to excess. "He has more technique than anybody at school."

"You would be impressed by anyone who could tongue sixteenth notes," Richter said to Jerry as he turned back to his work, nodding curtly to me.

Now it was quiet in the shop. I could hear a clock ticking loudly. After a while, trying to make intelligent conversation, I wondered aloud why clarinet players did not make their own reeds, the way oboe players did. Richter pushed back in his chair, took a puff on his pipe, looked me in the eye, and said, "In my orchestra, the flute player would be the lowest paid."

There was some laughter after this remark, but Richter did not join in it. Secretly, I was thrilled to have been included in Richter's orchestra, however generically.

Toward the end of our four years in the music school, Jerry and I played together in one of the city's opera orchestras, earning almost enough money to support ourselves. I often thought of what Richter had said to Jerry, because in moments when the notes were fast and difficult, he could be relied upon to be cleaning his instrument with a feather, or tugging at the thread on a reed. On the other hand, he was always ready for his solos. Oboe solos in the operas, it seemed to me, were always the loveliest melodies, and they were easy to play. My solos, on the other hand, were frequently tortuously difficult and tended to chirp and chatter. But we remained close friends, calling the melodic lines we played together, usually in octaves with the flute above, "floboe licks." There was considerable challenge in trying to match the cranky intonation of the oboe, an instrument with such a distinct and prominent sound, its wrongs were always right.

"Take care of my dog," Jerry would say, "I'm going to be on the West Coast for a week." (His teacher was always getting him special work, once even a summer in Peru.)

"I don't know anything about dogs, and besides, I have to practice."

"You'll be great at it. All you have to do is take him for a walk in the morning. Clair will clean up the shit." Clair was Jerry's girlfriend. The dog was a Great Dane which I outweighed by at least five pounds. Jerry had once shown me teeth marks on his oboe. I was afraid of the huge animal, but I let it pull me up and down Walnut Street each day. I bumped into Clair occasionally at Jerry's apartment. She filled a large garbage can with the excrement and chewed items and lugged it downstairs. One time she stopped me in the hallway after I had locked in the dog, Bubbles. It was dark and she rubbed against me and dug her fingers into my backside.

"Why don't we do it, right here in the hall," she whispered.

"Christ, Clair, give me a break."

"Go on then. You'd just tell Zoe anyway. You're no fun."

She was always doing stuff like that. Even when Jerry was around.

Zoe was my girlfriend. We had been together for nearly three years, and we almost lived together. At least she had a lot of her clothes in my apartment.

This was the year I would graduate, and my teacher had already talked to me about the orchestras I might have a reasonable chance of playing in, when my bad luck came. In my home state, the draft pool had run low, leaving nobody but the educationally deferred. My mother called and told me her friend, the red-haired lady in the basement of the courthouse, had told her I was sure to go soon, that it was extremely unlikely I would last the year. Suddenly for me, as for many of my high-school friends before, the world became very small.

I went to Washington, D.C., with Jerry to audition for service bands. It was Jerry's idea. He said it was a good job, and the best way he could think of to wait out the war.

The night before, Zoe and I had argued about it.

"James, there is this guy my sister knows. He's a psychiatrist. You can go to see him and he'll say you're gay or something."

"I don't know. What if he really doesn't do things like that? What if he turned me in? Besides, it's wrong."

"Isn't the war wrong?"

"Of course the war is wrong, but I've got to try to do the right thing."

"James, the right thing for you is what you're least afraid of."

I slammed the door and walked clear to the Art Museum before turning around. When I got back, Zoe had taken a cab home. She had also washed the dishes.

In Washington we auditioned for the Navy Band first. There are some things you are never prepared for. We heard the familiar strains of the B-flat Tchaikovsky Piano Concerto being played by two accordions and band. I didn't know whether to laugh or cry. Later I played for the Marine Band. It seemed somehow more professional. There were no accordions in evidence. And there was no basic training.

Jerry took the train back to Philadelphia after the first audition, muttering about how ridiculous it all was and accusing me of idiocy, but I had become determined. It seemed to me by that time that the whole adventure had been my own idea. When I was invited to join the Marine Band, I accepted. The arrangement was a bit odd. There was no contract, nothing in writing. First I was to enlist as a regular Marine. They would give me a three-month deferment, which would allow me to finish school. Then my orders were to report to Parris Island, South Carolina, and basic training (or, as I saw it, Parris Island and certain death). Sometime during that three-month waiting period, my orders would be changed, and I would be assigned to Marine Barracks in Washington, D.C., to make music, not war.

That spring found me desperate, still postmarked for Parris Island. I had been given a number I could call collect.

"Oh yeah, Baxter. Just a minute."

I was in a phone booth on Sansom Street watching delivery trucks grind by.

"Baxter. Baxter. Nope. Your orders haven't cleared yet, but there's a little time left. Don't worry, we haven't lost one of you guys yet. Well, we did lose one last October, but that wasn't my fault. Just call me tomorrow, and I'll probably have something." Sometimes the reassurances were smoother, sometimes not.

I looked over my first real apartment, a third-floor walkup on Pine Street, with its tiny round slatted table and matched chairs and grand four-poster bed I had bought from a graduating classmate for $50, the symbols of my ascendancy. And, of course, there were the books. I had two walls of books; only a few days before, I had sold a double flute case to buy the complete edition of Thoreau's *Journals*.

As I considered the job ahead of me, my crowded little efficiency did not seem so much a bachelor lair with socks hanging from the picture frames as a cozy little home I had made for myself. However, my lease was up. I daydreamed for a while about the adventures my little room had contained; but eventually, my thoughts returned to the present, and with grim energy, I packed the stuff up and moved it for storage into one of those apartment buildings entirely taken over by musicians. The place was deserted; most of the musicians, my friends from school, coming from better-stocked states, were already playing in orchestras or summer festivals. The sounds of brass players practicing from dawn to dusk were ghostly echoes; and, looking out a second-story window, I could see that the stain on the top of the ground-floor bakery's awning where a drunken cellist had once vomited was almost completely bleached away. I spread out a sleeping bag in that forest of musty furniture and stacked boxes and prepared to swelter and itch in lonely splendor. Between trips to the pay phone, I gave myself a mild case of tendinitis trying to support Mr. Thoreau's five-pound-plus lists of wildflowers. Even Jerry had deserted me. His deferment secure, he had gone on another of his teacher's international junkets.

Then I had a desperate idea. I would visit Zoe, who was somewhere in Maine, attending summer school. "Furthering her career," as she put it. Zoe was a singer. A coloratura soprano. All our plans about staying together, even of eventually getting married, had been, I suppose, a little like Clair on the staircase. We sort of meant it, but we didn't expect it to happen. Still, I had been surprised and hurt when Zoe told me after my Washington trip that she would not stay with me, that our relationship was over. I didn't plead with her. Somehow I think I felt she had abandoned her duty, and I was ashamed for her.

I had been phoning Washington for a week. It couldn't be any worse to call her.

She said, "Don't come."

I said I felt I must.

She said, "I won't have time to see you if you come."

But I was determined. I took the train and then rented a car, arriving too late at night to disturb anyone. I slept in the parking lot of the dormitory where she was staying. In the morning, I had her called down to the door, because I was not permitted inside. She scolded and fumed but agreed to allow me to pick her up at noon. When the time came, I took her to the dreary little cabin-row motel I had found. She immediately began undressing.

"Zoe, stop, I need to talk to you."

"I don't have time to talk to you, you bastard. I've got time to see that you get laid. That's all I've got to offer you. I know what you're going to say, anyway. You're going to start with one side of things, and when it's limp and chewed and covered with spit, then you're going to worry the other side. You're going to ask me to do the one thing I can't." And she began to cry. I tried to hold her.

"Don't you come near me with your clothes on. We're here to fuck. And your time's almost run out."

"Zoe, please. I don't know what's going to happen to me."

She finally let me hold her. And we did make love. She kept pulling at my clothes with the tears streaming down her face, clawing at me. Afterward I stroked her hair until she stopped crying. The bed was small and sagged in the middle as if it were trying to keep us together.

But then something seemed to click, and she began dressing.

"I can't help you now. I am going to pay attention to my life, my career. Whatever it may amount to, whatever insignificant little bit, it will be my life. Please take me back to the campus. I have a class."

I dropped her off and watched her walk away. She said, "Goodbye, James, good luck." She didn't kiss me or touch me or anything. She just walked away.

On the train to the city I thought of the old wood flute she had given me. It had been very early on in our relationship. I think she just happened upon it in an antique store on Pine Street. It was a perfect example of her extravagance and impulsiveness. I hadn't accepted it in very good grace. I remember grousing about how junky it looked and how she had probably been swindled. She would never tell me how much she paid for it. Nevertheless, I kept it. I knew I had hurt her feelings, and I had always meant to fix it up, to try to make it playable. Maybe if I worked on that flute I could pass the time without going crazy. I have always been pretty good with my hands. When I was a kid I used to take my fishing reels apart all the time, and they were nearly as complicated as clocks. I remembered how peaceful I felt, lining up the cogs and gears on a TV tray, how the hours passed unnoticed until my mother scolded me to go outside and play.

When I got home and looked it over, I realized the old flute was in terrible shape, so I took it to Richter's shop and asked him for suggestions. I was still afraid of him. I could picture him scowling over his half glasses. There were strategically located warts and wens which gave him a kind of diabolical authority. To my surprise, the old man invited me to spend the week in his shop, working on my flute. He would give me a few pointers, and I could sit at his assistant's place, who was on vacation. The first day I stayed well into the night, not really working much, but watching the old man as he worked on a flute, taking off the keys, making a fine adjustment with a tiny crescent of paper under the pad, then replacing the keys, and testing the flute. The paper he used for adjustments was from the yellow pages, and he counseled me to use paper from the meat section—I would be unlikely to regret the page I had removed. He had a row of small pipes which he constantly smoked. I brought out my pipe and we joined in filling the room to the limits of its shadows with obnoxious clouds of Walnut Blend. Every tobacco can he had ever bought seemed to be stacked along the walls, unmarked, but filled with keys and rods, washers and pads, and with hundreds of other impossibly arcane, outdated objects that might become useful some day. The next morning, I was not particularly surprised when a man walked into our mutual mushroom cloud holding a lighted cigarette, and Richter ordered him out of the room. He could not abide the smell of cigarette tobacco.

I realized that without Richter's assistant on duty, there were going to be some things I might need to do to be helpful, but I did not suspect they might require clairvoyance. There was an old black plastic radio with a broken dial on a shelf, along with hundreds of cigar boxes. The radio was tuned to the classical music station, the boxes were filled with pads. Pads for clarinets, pads for flutes, for bassoons, for oboes. And other things. Paper of varying thickness for shims, cork, leather, clock oil, cork grease . . . and dust, black city dust, white plaster dust, tobacco dust, anonymous dust, some of it feathery as moth-antennae, some of it hard as cement. Richter would be hunched over his bench, working intently, and turn suddenly to me, saying, "Give me that box," gesturing vaguely toward the wall with the hundred cigar boxes. I would leap up and reach uncertainly toward any of them. "No, not that one." If I was lucky, I would get it on the third try, my psychic triangulation aided by the growing impatience in the master's voice.

At lunchtime the old man would put down his work, take a

sandwich and an apple from a paper bag, eat, then, putting his head on his arms, sleep for twenty minutes. No one spoke, no one disturbed him, and a wise customer it was who found some place else to be during this sacred ritual. I would rest, too, and in exactly twenty minutes Richter would raise his head, light the last pipe in the little row, tamping down the dottle, then pump out blue clouds of hallucinogenic smoke, which seemed reluctant to rise much above his head. We talked little, but when we did, it was usually of music. I could identify some of the more obscure pieces that came on the radio, and that pleased him. He told me once about his home in Germany, a little town where everybody made instruments, clarinets, oboes, and bassoons. He had made his own flute himself, of silver, some thirty years before. It seemed sturdier than necessary, but he gripped it with awesome strength. While he played poorly, he seemed to enjoy the flute more than the other instruments, which he played to test their function, not to make music. It was with a fearsome licking and pursing that he prepared his embouchure for a recreational toot on that heavyweight tube, which always reminded me more of something made by Smith and Wesson than a master woodwind craftsman. He was fond of maps, and, forgetful in this one thing, repeatedly made me show him my home state in the Midwest, a lonely, leaning rectangle almost lost in the center of a large U.S. wall map which had suffered more than its share from the leaking skylight. Once I watched him crush the open end of an alto flute headjoint like a beer can with a careless push against the worn, carved front of the workbench, then restore it so perfectly, the owner or the maker would never have known what had happened. I banged my head on that work bench several times as well, on hands and knees, sweeping with a hand brush to help him find a tiny screw he had dropped.

We improvised the tools I would need. The best one was a testing device made from the cap of a lipstick with a pad seat soldered to the end, so I could see if the pad was good by trying to suck air through it. (Richter showed me how he used his version of this tool to test a pad. The pad was good if the suction was strong enough to stick his end of the tube to his lower lip and pull it out grotesquely, until it released with a loud pop. If the pop was loud enough, the pad was sound.)

Once, toward the end of the week, Richter said, "So James, how will you like this Marine Band?" He didn't look up from a piece of keywork he was filing.

"There was this guy who played one time in the flute section of the opera orchestra. He was terrible, but somebody said that he was a good player until he went into the Army. After three years he lost it. That's what I'm really afraid of."

"You will stop practicing in this band?" He looked at me over his glasses.

"I guess not," I said.

"Then, someday you will play in an orchestra like this one." He gestured triumphantly toward the radio, which was playing a Brahms symphony. I realized that for him the orchestra was in the room with us. For me it was a plastic radio with a broken dial, and the music was coming from a little cone of cardboard with a magnet behind it. But the matter was closed. I would practice and endure.

I spent most of the week with the pads off the flute, and a strange naked thing it was, like a tube of Swiss cheese, seeming nearly all holes. The keys gave it dignity, if nothing else. After a week's work, and with Richter's help, my old flute was good for only three notes, and those from the top joint, before the accumulated error of warped wood and nicks in the tone holes muffled the sound hopelessly. The sound was pure, but with a hint of richness, like the low notes of a clarinet. The cracks and warping of age had made it impossible for the lower notes to sound. I was disappointed. I had been sure that Richter could save it. When he looked at it the last time, he shrugged.

"It's an old flute. Nothing is so hopeless. Usually the head-joints crack. See." He pointed to a row of cracked wooden head-joints at the back of the bench. I had not noticed them before. Some had had a metal core and the wood had shrunk, splitting terribly. Others had only partial cracks, but in every case, the cracks were fatal, running through the embouchure holes.

"Why do you keep them?"

"Oh, they might be of some use. Like your flute. You will keep your flute?" He looked at me over his glasses again.

"Yes, I'll keep the flute," I said.

The last day before Parris Island, my orders came. I said goodbye to Richter, and left his little junkyard of a shop with my tools and my flute, carrying with me the strangest feeling, almost of exultation—as if my picture were now among those grainy photographs of mustached and bearded musicians, all of us staring into the dark room with mysterious gray eyes.

I walked down the creaking stairs and took the train to Washington. I did not know how lonely I would feel, or that later, almost a year later, Clair would call me from National Airport, having missed her plane, and that we would try to make love on top of my flimsy table, and that it would collapse, and that later the bed would collapse, and that we would laugh until we cried. I did not know when I walked down those stairs that I would rent an apartment in Arlington, Virginia, or that I would eat my meals austerely in an empty room with a single chair for a table, my mind blank as the newly painted walls, until a rainy afternoon two months after my arrival, as if to signal the seeding of my new life, when my lost furniture would be finally delivered in an enormous crate, on a flatbed truck, and the workmen would pry open one side, and let it all slide out, books first, slowly, into the mud and rain.

Leopard-Skin
Pill-Box Hat

Washington, D.C., 1968

I drove like a crazy man in those days. Ever since that first time in the locked ward, I felt I had a right. Police never stopped me, and despite my indifference I couldn't seem to stray from the road. When someone suggested I was tempting fate (and this happened on a regular basis), I would stare blankly and pretend I didn't get it. Once I backed into the only tree in the parking lot of my apartment building, thinking about that flat-chested secretary who wouldn't return my calls. Women were worse than distracting, they were hazardous, I thought, as I pounded the steering wheel. Why would a woman go to bed with you once and then just pretend you never existed?

"Don't ask." I could hear the voice in my head in Franklin's comic inflections.

"You shouldn't ask." My friend Franklin said stay away from those young girls, they don't wash themselves and they don't know how to fuck. Franklin had a way of making the best of a bad situation. Franklin was a jazz drummer who wanted to learn to play the flute. All he seemed to do was stay home, practice the flute, and cook. His girlfriend Lucy had a job in an office somewhere downtown where she apparently made enough to keep things together. Franklin and I hung out when I wasn't marching and playing band concerts. We drank a lot of beer together.

I met Franklin when he answered an ad about a wood flute I was selling, an old one that didn't work very well. It turned out he had an old wood flute, too. It seems like everybody's got an old wood flute in the attic. Franklin insisted he wanted lessons. From me. An unlikely mentor. Frequently stoned. A cultivator of closet-grown marijuana. A consumer of Columbian and Mexican grass, of blossoms, of brown hash, black hash, mushrooms. Occasionally LSD and amphetamines. I had joined the Marine Band to escape Vietnam and, having accomplished that end, was at a loss. So I gave Franklin flute lessons. But it was always the same.

"Play some notes, Franklin. Warm up."

Franklin would play his tuning A three times, then lapse into "Night and Day."

"God damn it, James. I can't play shit without thinking of some stupid tune."

"It's a good tune, Franklin. Why don't you just go ahead and warm up?" It was hopeless. Franklin would think of another tune, stomp around swearing, and before long it would be time to go out and get more beer. Franklin did not much approve of dope, but he would smoke a joint now and then to be sociable. Beer was his vice. We drank it slowly, but relentlessly, pausing in our long rambling discussions of life, sex, and music only to piss loudly behind the thin door of Franklin's bathroom. Franklin lined the beer bottles up against the wall and toward midnight would marvel at them. "Look at that, James. Can you imagine that two skinny guys could have put away so much beer?" (Only in Franklin's mind was Franklin skinny.) "This is a phenomenon. There is a portent in this. We are drawing astral nourishment.

This is not the mere consumption of a beverage." And he would go on, raising his voice so Lucy and I could hear him in the bathroom.

"What would you like to hear, Jimmy?" Lucy was in charge of music.

"I'd like to hear Bartók. The Czech Philharmonic, please. They have the world's loudest flute player. A wood flute, too. Puffs his cheeks like Dizzy Gillespie."

"How about the Beatles?"

"That's fine."

Lucy sat down beside me. "Just don't admire Ringo's drumming, okay? Remember how pissed off Franklin gets?"

Franklin from the bathroom. "I heard that."

Lucy sighed and headed to the kitchen. Franklin paused on his way from the bathroom to the divan and theatrically admired Lucy's departure.

"A fine woman, James. A fine woman."

Franklin enjoyed life. And I enjoyed the time I spent with Franklin. As much as I could remember. I would lose a week, sometimes a month. I'd be there, driving eighty in the tunnels under the circles and showing up in my ridiculous uniform at Marine Barracks for work, such as it was. I knew, or thought I knew, that my friends were taking care of me. It was a lot like swimming under water in the big lake when I was a kid. The water was warm and there was a safe green glow from the sun and waves above, but if you got too deep, the water turned black and cold, and you would panic and wonder if you could ever get up to the air. But when you did, you'd cough and spit a little, and then forget the whole business until the next time.

Franklin introduced me to Hobbs. And Hobbs said read *Steppenwolf*. So I read *Steppenwolf*. I couldn't remember what I had read, but I had read it to please a friend. It was just that Hobbs was so irritating. He loved to talk at me. He didn't talk to me, he probably didn't talk *to* anybody. I complained to Lucy, who was a better listener than Franklin, that Hobbs was one confusing son of a bitch. But Lucy just ran her fingers through my hair in a motherly way.

Hobbs had wavy brown hair, the perfectly round glasses which came with the decade, and an Adam's apple which played under the pale skin of his prominent neck like a squirrel chasing its tail around a tree, while little mortars containing fragments of "the magic theater" and "the heartless hegemony of music" burst harmlessly around him. Sometimes I would try to talk gibberish back to Hobbs. And Hobbs would say, "You're absolutely right. You're absolutely right." Then he'd stare at me in triumph as if the two of us had invented penicillin. And I would wonder, "What did I say?"

Everyone I knew in those days was a friend of Franklin's. There were Barney and Elsie, for example. Elsie was an actress, an ample woman, overflowing with warm sweet-smelling flesh, dim as a stone, but, for me, always an active source of sexual torture. Barney was a photographer, and the triumph of his art was a black-and-white photograph of Elsie's ass, blown up to the size of Mt. Rushmore and prominently displayed in Barney's apartment one floor up from Franklin's. Barney and Elsie were around most of the time. A lot of people came and went, but it was Hobbs who thought to match me up with Anna. Later I decided that Hobbs must have thought of her because she was crazy, too.

I can see Hobbs and Franklin at that fateful moment. No doubt listening to Dylan. *Blond on Blond.* After Hesse, Hobbs is nuts on Bob Dylan. They are probably listening to "Stuck Inside of Mobile with the Memphis Blues Again." During this scene I am at Marine Barracks, standing inspection, and having forgotten to slick my hair down with water so it will look like I don't need a haircut, getting stuck with a week of library duty. Franklin says, "James almost wrecked his car because he's so horny." And Hobbs quotes *Steppenwolf* so long that Franklin takes a trip to the john. But then, about the time Franklin is coming out, Hobbs says, "I know, I'll fix him up with Anna." And Franklin says, "Who's Anna?" And Hobbs begins to confuse even Franklin, whose thought is slow, but thorough, like spilled molasses.

I have imagined this scene many times, and at the words "Who's Anna?" my mind trails off, and all I can hear is Dylan, really getting down and desperate, "Oh, Mama, can this really be the end . . ."

I had been on enough blind dates to have low expectations. But I was curious to see who Hobbs thought would be a good match for me. There were six people crowded around a table for four, Barney and Elsie, Hobbs and his girlfriend, a quiet girl, dedicated to listening. I am sure she didn't speak a word that evening. How could she have? She was Hobbs's date. And then there was Anna. Anna had long black hair, dark eyes, and a sweet smile. She seemed in the midst of all that happened absurdly calm and peaceful. We had gone to a nightclub to hear a group of Spanish guitarists that Barney knew, and the room was frantic, noisy . . .

I tried to listen to the music, but Hobbs kept shouting in my ear, telling me why "She takes just like a woman, she makes love just like a woman, and she aches just like a woman, but she breaks just like a little girl" meant something about pre-mythic animism, when I noticed a large Spaniard under the table. He was one of the guitarists on a break and, only a moment ago, he had been wedged across the table, talking to Anna. I had imagined the Spaniard knew Anna, but when I saw him give her a note scribbled on yellow paper I realized the situation. "Fine," I thought. "Anna is handling this just dandy, two dates in one night. This is the guy Barney told me about before. That he doesn't use a jack to change a tire on his car. He just picks it up and puts it on a rock." Now what was he doing? Yes, he was under the table, attempting to kiss Anna's toes.

I asked Anna if she was ready to leave. Hobbs seemed insulted. I was terrified of the bear under the table. But wait. The bear seemed to have passed out. Anna was ready to leave anyway. Hobbs was stuck in his seat. He wasn't able to climb out over the bear, so Anna and I snaked along through much jangling, stomping, and strumming on our way to the door and the explosively quiet night outside.

On the way to the car, Anna took my hand and smiled at me. I had parked several blocks away, and for a while nobody said anything. It was nice holding her hand.

Anna stopped in front of me.

"I'm sorry about what happened tonight. It wasn't really a good place to talk." She gave me a quick little kiss.

I took courage. "My apartment is under the main flight path for National Airport. But it's quiet this time of night. We could talk there."

Anna nodded (I hadn't expected this), and we went to my place in Arlington.

What did we say? I ransacked my mind afterward. It was slow coming, but this is what I could remember. Anna told me she had five brothers and sisters. Sam, Sandra, Sally, Sonya, and Sinclair. Not the sort of thing I would have forgotten if I had wanted to. Anna was her middle name. Something with an S. She didn't care to say. Did I mind? I didn't mind. I told her I got up every morning, made coffee, and wrote a poem. That I put the poem in a drawer and never looked at it again. But then I recited one. "Hail to the hedgehog, short and fat—he don't know where his rear end's at." And Anna pinched me. Hard. I had a bruise the next day. I had learned an important rule. Anna's Rule. No humor. She didn't seem mad at me personally. I must have brought out a little dope. I smoked it in a pipe because I didn't smoke cigarettes, and in those days I didn't know how to roll a joint. Then I remembered the Yeats poem about the fairies stealing a child away for her . . .

> Come away, O human child!
> To the waters and the wild
> With a faery, hand in hand,
> For the world's more full of weeping than you can
> understand.

I told her that when I got high I felt like a leaf spinning on a little stream, that I could look up and see the ferns bending down from the bank, nearly touching the water. That sometimes I felt I lived in that poem about the fairies. Anna was looking at my books. She took down a copy of *Winnie-the-Pooh*.

"Do you like this?"

"I'll have to confess that I've never read it. My grandmother gave it to me just before she died. She had a lot of books for her grandchildren."

"I'll read it to you. There are poems, too. I know you'll like them."

Somehow it didn't seem like such a bad idea to me. We were sitting on the divan and Anna said, "I want to do something nice for you," and she began to unzip my fly and bend over my lap. I remember thinking that there must be something wrong, that this shouldn't be happening to me on a first date. (It had never happened to me before on any kind of date.) But in a while, when my heart started beating again, I was hugging and kissing her in hysterical gratitude. I would have kissed her toes like the bear if she had let me.

I began to see Anna regularly. Mostly at her place. I would meet her at school where she was an art student, and we would pick up some groceries and a bottle of California wine. Her apartment was in the back of a large house in a nice residential section with enormous trees. The land sloped down steeply past the back of the house, but the trees just kept getting taller. You could look out her kitchen window and see a space like a redwood forest— or so I liked to imagine. It was quiet. Even the birds seemed uncomfortable in that cathedral-like yard, and inside, Anna had painted everything in white and flat black. Mostly flat black. We would eat by candlelight, then make love on the floor. I felt like a monk there, except when we made love.

I took Anna to Franklin's one evening for dinner, and Franklin had a bottle of rye whiskey. There was much instructional verbiage from Franklin, and we all had a fair amount to drink. Lucy seemed particularly cheerful. When Franklin brought out the sesame tahini, chickpeas, and garlic and began flailing around with a huge knife in ceremonial preparation for making hummus, Lucy asked us if we had heard the barkle story.

"Franklin and I were living in a little trailer court in West Virginia. We hadn't been together long, and he wanted to fix me some special dish, I don't remember what. We went to this little store with a Coca-Cola sign on the screen door, and Franklin asked them for garlic, and this old man said 'What,' and Franklin said, 'Garlic, garlic,' and the old guy said, 'You must not be from around here,' and Franklin said, 'I just want garlic, G-A-R-L-I-C,' and the guy said 'Oh, you mean barkles,' and he gave us the garlic. It's the only time I've known Franklin to be speechless."

I laughed and Anna gave me another hard pinch. It was like a bee sting. I pretended it didn't hurt, but I spilled my drink on her, and then she laughed until she coughed, and Lucy put on "John Wesley Harding," and Franklin cut his finger.

When the evening was over, back at Anna's place, I asked her why she had pinched me.

"I don't know, Jimmy. I'm sorry."

She got up and started watering her plants.

"Things happen too quickly sometimes. I really don't know why I do it. Do you mind much?"

I thought for a while, then ventured carefully, "It isn't so much that I mind, but that I don't understand what is going on."

"When you laugh . . . when people laugh, it's like they're laughing at me. No . . . it's like . . . what do you feel like when you perform, when you get on the stage in front of people?"

"It feels good. It feels good if I think they can hear me playing . . . otherwise . . . if I'm just there for them to look at, like in the band, I feel as if I am being jerked around."

" 'Jerked around' is when somebody else is doing what he wants to do, only you're doing it for him?"

"Yeah, that's about it."

"Well, when people laugh at a joke, it's almost always because somebody is a joke, somebody doesn't understand. When I was little, my father had me tell this polar-bear joke. Everybody always laughed, and I thought it was nice. Picture me, parading out before company in my yellow dress."

She began in a kind of sing-song voice.

" 'How to catch a polar bear. First dig a hole in the ice. Then you scatter peas around the hole. When the polar bear comes to take a pea, you kick him in the ice hole.' I told it dozens of times, and then one day, I got it. They were laughing at me. I didn't like it. I don't like it. I just don't like jokes."

I just gave her a hug. At any time before in my life I would have had something to say about polar bears.

Anna and I had been together for perhaps a month, and things were going well. I spent most of my time with her. Sometimes we would just lie together in the candle light, tracing each other's hip bones with our fingers, moving gradually into more lovemaking. We seldom talked. And then one evening the phone rang.

Anna came out of the kitchen where the phone was and said, "I have to go identify my father's body. Mother won't do it. They said any time tomorrow morning."

All I knew about Anna's parents was that her mother lived somewhere in the city (Anna didn't seem keen on introducing me), most of the S's were out of the nest, and that, apart from the polar-bear business, there had been no mention of her father.

So I said it. "Why won't your mother go? What happened, for God's sake?"

"She divorced him years ago. He's crazy. They found him in a park in Manassas. He had had a heart attack. They called Mother and she told them to call me. Here's the address where he is." She handed me a piece of paper with the address.

"You don't have to do it."

"Mother won't do it."

"Why won't she do it?"

"He was feeding the pigeons."

That was it. No more talk.

The next morning was a beautiful spring Saturday. I drove Anna to Manassas and it was windy. The car kept getting blown over the center lane. The radio was on and Dylan was there. He was everywhere.

Well I see you got your brand new leopard-skin pill-box hat,
Well, you must tell me, baby,
How your head feels under somethin' like that,
Under your brand new leopard-skin pill-box hat.

The morgue, or whatever it was, was in a little park with rows of daffodils tossing in the wind. I asked Anna if she wanted me to go in with her and she said she didn't mind. I had expected something like the city morgues in the movies with giant drawers and toe tags. But there was just a room, like a doctor's office, and there was Anna's father, in the middle. He looked fine. Fine for a dead guy, I thought. Even, I supposed, for a live guy. He had on a sailor suit, which was a little weird, but he had a nicely trimmed beard, and he just didn't look dead. We sat down afterward with an envelope which contained his personal effects. He had some pills (unidentified), an old pocketknife with a dirty wood handle, and a wallet—no credit cards, just a few dollars and coins. Anna signed some papers so he could be cremated, and we drove home. We stopped in a diner and ordered coffee and sat and stared at the rings the water glasses made on the table.

"He used to lock the door and we had to play outside. Even when I was little. I used to sit in the street and eat dirt."

"Do you remember that?"

"I think so. My sister told me. Sometimes it was cold, but we had to stay outside."

"Why?"

Anna just drew with her finger in the rings the water glasses made. Outside, the wind was blowing harder. Some kind of bad weather coming in.

Anna's face began to twist in anguish. I couldn't imagine what she was thinking.

"Why the sailor suit?" I asked absurdly.

Anna began to speak, but I could not hear what she was saying. I leaned toward her as far as I could, realizing that whatever she was saying was being wrenched from the most painful hiding place I could imagine. She went on, but she was crying, and it was impossible to understand what she was saying. When she stopped, I handed her my glass of water and she drank it. I couldn't ask her what she had told me. I decided it didn't matter. All that mattered was that she had told me.

The one thing I hadn't told Anna about was my stay in the big Navy hospital in Bethesda. Franklin and Lucy knew. Probably Hobbs. I had had a destructive episode in a parking lot and had bloodied both arms and fists smashing windshields. It seemed more than ludicrous to me that the Navy began dealing with my problem by giving me drugs. A lot of the guys I met in the locked ward were Marines who had for some reason confused a member of their own chain of command with the enemy. I found most of their reasons quite sane to my way of thinking. After a few weeks I was given into the custody of a Navy psychiatrist, Dr. Stevens, and I still reported for weekly sessions. Dr. Stevens often talked about his wish to be a Navy flyer with a flowing scarf, and seemed obsessed with memories of his "Daddy." I could not help thinking that he was in the right line of work. It was Dr. Stevens's job to make a good soldier of me, and I did work at keeping the rules of my job. I had seen something of the real war in the hospital, of its toll. My own part in it now seemed less unlucky.

When I brought Anna back from Manassas, she said she needed to be alone. I went home to my apartment for the first time in several days. I am not very clear about what followed. Probably there would have been no sleeping for me anyway. My desk drawer contained all sorts of amphetamines, and in the corner of the bedroom there was a kit for building a harpsichord, hardly begun. At Marine Barracks there is roll call every morning, but unless someone takes the trouble to come get you, you can work undisturbed. Your mind might be filled with daffodils waving in the wind or visions of a corpse in a sailor suit with a neatly trimmed beard. But more likely it is empty, mercifully empty. Franklin might have called or dropped by, but Franklin was working on a novel, his latest enthusiasm. Finally it was Hobbs who came around and found me stacking and unstacking the little pieces of cherry wood that go on the keyboard. Hobbs called downtown and soon there was a driver and I was delivered to Bethesda for another week in the locked ward, listening to the screams of the crazed and enraged, and the panicked footfall of beardless corpsmen running with mattresses, the only effective shields against such pure violence. And it wasn't long before I felt better, but Dr. Stevens was severely disappointed and resigned from the case. My case was now in the hands of a psychiatrist with an extremely thick German accent, who suggested that my problems might be solved by a discharge from the Marine Corps.

"Don't kid me, Adolph," I replied, but Dr. Redisch seemed to be serious. All I had to do was check in with Redisch's staff twice a week while my papers cleared.

I picked my way through the scattered pieces of my yet-to-be-assembled harpsichord and found the phone. Franklin was home, but he did not seem glad to hear from me. He said that Hobbs had been by, and that Anna wasn't doing well. Anna? It was like waking up. I had a terrible feeling. I drove to her house and knocked on the door. There wasn't any answer. The curtains were pulled, so I couldn't see inside. I had the feeling she might be there, so I walked around the neighborhood for a while and came back to knock every quarter hour or so. Knocking and calling.

It was my fourth attempt and I had already stopped knocking. I was looking at the tall trees, wondering why anyone would call garlic barkles, when I heard Anna call very faintly, "Go away, Jimmy."

Oddly enough, I felt a strong desire to walk away, as if I hadn't heard her, but she knew I was there, and she had asked me to go away, which meant she really wanted me to stay. It all seemed obvious. My mind began to spin. What should I say? Should I say, "Anna, I'm going to have to break the door down"? Should I say, "Anna, I've been in the hospital, they just let me out"? Or "Let me in, let me in, by the hair of my chin"? I was beginning to warm to the Three Pigs approach when Anna opened the door.

I stood there for a second, confused and disappointed. Anna looked gaunt, beautiful. Then it just came out.

"Let me in, let me in," I said.

"Not by the hair of your chinny, chin, chin," she said, and she didn't smile.

So I went in, and closed the door behind me. We sat down on the floor in the black-and-white room.

"I've been away."

"Whatever you say."

She still wasn't smiling. It occurred to me that I had already known out in the redwood forest that there was not going to be any lovemaking.

"Away with us she's going, the solemn-eyed . . ."

"The what?"

"She'll hear no more the lowing of the calves on the warm hillside or the kettle on the hob . . ."

"Anna, why are you quoting Yeats at me?"

"Ernest was an elephant, a great big fellow, Leonard was a lion with a six-foot tail, George was a goat, and his beard was yellow and James . . ."

"Anna."

". . . was a very small snail."

"Anna. Stop it." I was thinking about shaking her. Did people really do things like that?

Then she smiled at me. "I'm going away, Jimmy. I'm going away. You'll never see me again. To the waters and the wild with a faery, hand in hand."

"Don't go," I said, thinking, "Go ahead, go ahead. What am I doing here?"

"I'm going in a boat, and when they get to where they're going, there'll be no, no Anna."

Then she crawled across the floor toward me. We had been sitting on opposite sides of the room, as if we were afraid of each other. For a moment I thought she was going to start up, and in spite of myself, I started to get excited. But she just looked at me and said, "Now you can go."

I got up, then took her hands and pulled her up, too. She didn't seem to want to get up, but she did. She let me embrace her. I wasn't excited anymore. But now I wanted to stay.

She seemed to understand. "Go, Jimmy."

And that worked. I turned around and walked out the door.

I sat in my car with my hands on the steering wheel, not thinking for a while. Then I said aloud, "What would I do, if I knew what to do?" I closed my eyes and felt how warm the steering wheel was in my hands. It felt good. My hands had gotten cold in Anna's house. I thought of the harpsichord. I reached to put the key in the ignition. Then I stopped, got out of the car briskly, and walked to the drugstore about a block away, where there was an old phone booth in the back. I pulled the door shut and sat there with my eyes closed again. I knew if I really concentrated I could do it. It was an ordinary name. Too ordinary. Jones! Anna had been seeing a psychiatrist—a woman named Jones. I called three area hospitals before I located a resident psychiatrist who fit my description. I said it was an emergency and left my number. Then I drove home and connected my phone. I made coffee and did some housecleaning. I threw away quite a lot of unmatched socks. I threw away the photograph of Elsie's ass Barney had given me when he got a new girlfriend. Then I scraped the pills out of the pencil rack in my desk drawer and flushed them down the toilet. Around sunset Dr. Jones called, and I told her about Anna. I said

I was Anna's friend and that I judged myself to be an unreliable source, but I had the feeling . . . Dr. Jones seemed to have the feeling, too. Dr. Jones and Mr. Dr. Jones met me at Anna's house and Mr. Dr. and I talked about basketball under a street light for almost an hour while Dr. Jones talked with Anna. Then Dr. Jones came out and told me I should go home, that Anna had decided to check into the hospital, that she did not want . . . it would be best if . . . if I did not talk to her now, etc. So I went home (driving slowly and thoughtfully) and slept until I was wakened at midday by a pair of mockingbirds singing in thirds.

What do I remember? Delirious hours of pushing the waxing machine on the locked wards. In and out of little pools of sunlight. Ah that thorazine. Tricycles squeaking outside while I stacked the cherry-wood keys of my harpsichord. Elsie's ass. Sometimes the mockingbirds sang all night. They'd wake me at three or four in the morning.

I got my discharge papers, and I was hanging out, thinking about getting a job. I was practicing again. I'd even made a few phone calls. Then one day I got a call from Lucy. She asked me to come over and talk.

When I got there there was no Franklin.

"Where's Franklin?" I asked.

"He's thinking about moving to Ireland," Lucy said.

I looked hard at Lucy. Lucy *was* a fine woman. A handsome woman. Lucy came from West Virginia and probably knew how to milk cows. Franklin said as much once. It's just that Lucy was moody. I could tell what was coming. I could feel it in the worst place. It was a divining rod.

Lucy told me that all this time she had had a special feeling about me, and that it had just gotten stronger and stronger. It had come between her and Franklin. She wanted to do for me.

It seemed so quiet in that room without Franklin. Just me and Lucy and all that lust. I started noticing things around me. Little cracks in the plaster. Franklin's flute case. He must not have moved out yet.

Lucy looked awfully unhappy.

"I just had to tell you this," she said. "I hope you don't mind."

I imagined being in a blissful sweaty tangle with Lucy. I stood up from the table.

"I'm leaving town," I said. It was news to me. "I just got a job back in Philadelphia. This is just one of those things that happened at the wrong time. You don't know how sorry I am."

Lucy looked like she was going to cry. I left then, and when I got into my car, tears began to slide down my cheeks. I thought of Lucy and Franklin, of the warm yellow light in Franklin's kitchen. I thought of Anna. Anna needed to get well. I needed to get straight.

I got a call about a job in the next day or so. It wasn't in Philadelphia, but it was a real job, playing new music in Buffalo. Things often work out that way. So I invited Hobbs over and gave him my record player. It wasn't much, an old AR, scuffed and covered with dust-coated drops of honey I'd spilled when I was stoned, but I wanted to do something for Hobbs. We drank the last of my Black Jack and listened to Dylan. The music seemed oddly cheerful to me. The kind of music that later in my life I would choose for housecleaning, painting, window washing. But that day I listened to it quietly, earnestly, giving Hobbs his due.

Enlightenment

Philadelphia, Wisconsin, 1970

The sound I'm hearing, of Sally falling down the steps with the vacuum cleaner, is the sound of eviction. I'm not worried about Sally. It's hard to imagine anyone built like a pine cone suffering serious injury, but these are hard times for all of us. The war whoops of that visiting French-horn player haven't helped the situation much, and if a few of our friends didn't look quite so much like Charles Manson, we might have held out longer. Upper-class Philadelphia rations its brotherly love. Diane says everything is all right with Sally. Diane is our pianist—slender, birdlike, rapacious, carnivorous. You could drop a load of bricks two stories into a piano, and not get the volume, the intensity, the sexual energy she puts into the instrument when she plays. Her husband, David, on the other hand, is some kind of large chipmunk, a seed eater, a rummager of catalogues. They are an odd pair, but we are an odd assortment in an odd world. Diane is our link with respectability. She teaches at a distinguished music school. She performs with the Philadelphia Orchestra. She sees to our cuts and bruises. Anything pertaining to blood is hers.

Sally, when she is not engaging in one of her hysterical cleaning patrols, or falling down stairs, keeps mostly to her room. She's about ten months pregnant. We think the guru did it last summer. Anyway that's why the great schism. Why Sally and Thad stay in their room nearly all the time. There's not much togetherness here anymore. Diane is usually working and David has always wandered around by himself, eating sunflower seeds and reading the kind of stuff that gets stuck under the windshield wiper of your car. Harold sleeps a lot and listens surreptitiously outside my door when I am practicing. He is taking flute lessons with me, and I am his maestro du jour. It's a peculiar feeling, being listened to this way, but everything is peculiar and lonely here. This house has a way of losing people with its twenty-plus rooms.

This is an awkward time in my life. I am like the surface of a pond in early spring, full of shivers and indecisive winds, scribbles and blots, turnings and erasings—all prescience, prone to apparitions, memories, and forgettings. I am determined to learn something. The Big Something. The Meaning Of. I hardly know how to begin. It seems there's something called the Delancey Street Association, and we have run afoul of it.

"My husband, the Surgeon General . . ." When she deigns to speak to us at all, this is the preface to every sentence uttered by our neighbor to the east, who seems to *be* the Delancey Street Association. It is she who has managed this eviction, on the grounds that we have transformed a one-family dwelling into some kind of boarding house. Heavens, we would argue that we *are* one family, the seven of us. So what if we have as many factions and alliances as an Italian parliament? I think this is an identifying characteristic of any true family. It is our youth, our beards, our clothing, the dope we must certainly smoke, the loud music we play (I should say, the loud music we make, for we are nearly all musicians), that have brought us to this pass. But I am deeply resentful of this woman. This will have been my only adventure in communal living. My life is destined to become progressively more and more ordinary. The Pearl S. Buck Foundation to our west and Rudolph Serkin directly across the street did not complain. We have only a few weeks more to sort out our lives together before we drift apart.

Bump, bump, bump. How did we get here? Let me go back a bit. Yes, Diane is tending to Sally. David has come, too, bringing with him the calm of seed packets and old comic books.

It began with a summer music festival in Wisconsin. I had inherited the festival with the job I had just quit, principal flutist in a Southern orchestra. I had discovered the South was inhospitable to my rimless glasses and Woodstock-length hair. It was a place where too many folks said, "You play in a *sympathy* orchestra?" Anna had come there with me from Washington, D.C., and now we were thinking of moving to Philadelphia, where I had been a student. But moving time would coincide with that before-mentioned festival which had been founded by the conductor from whose orchestra I had just seceded.

"He'll fire you, James," Anna said. "You can't quit the lousy job and keep the good one. They go together."

And as usual Anna was right. He did fire me. But not until after that summer. I had already signed the contract. Anna pointed out to me that Slotkin was surely catching on to my tricks. When he asked for more expression I affected a billy-goat vibrato that would have been offensive in the thirties, the era of its popularity. I also tended to ask esoteric questions about the tuning of resultant tones. (Resultant tones are slight buzzings which are sometimes caused by the interaction of pitches of different frequencies but similar energy levels. They are probably about as audible to the audience as a second violinist's rumbling stomach.) A properly timed resultant-tone question could so distract Slotkin that the rehearsal might be delayed for twenty minutes while he experimented with different instrumental combinations, trying to hear the impossible buzzings himself.

". . . Philadelphia sounds nice. Of course I'll go with you. I don't mind. . . ." Anna was an artist. Painting, drawing, print making, sculpture, ceramics. She could not seem to decide what not to do. And why does she sound so, so flat? So agreeable? Because this is all I heard. And why is this all I heard? Because I was barely twenty years old. The instrument I was then did not register in the infra-red, the ultraviolet. I had no notion of the real Anna.

So now it's August. Anna and I have made it to Wisconsin. This is the guru-summer. We have rented a little cottage, and it's a week before the festival starts. We are very sweet together. We hold hands a lot and speak of imaginary creatures and doings known only to ourselves. It's all a bit peculiar, incestuous perhaps.

What else, then? Well, there was the poem, of course. I had already begun working on it, a page a day. It eventually grew to over two hundred pages, and I was to carry it around with me for years, like Morley's chain. The poem of enlightenment.

There is something about coincidence in youth. When met, this convergence of events becomes a sign from God. And so it was with me. Anna had been sent a box of strange books by an old friend, for whom there is no space in this story, and I had been imprinted, like a baby duck, by an enormous poem called *Savitri* written by the Indian sage Sri Aurobindo. This I believe, largely on the strength of my vague resemblance to the young man portrayed on the book jacket with his wispy ethereal beard. (I also felt I favored Hermann Hesse, but I could not find the floppy wide-brimmed hat he affected on the back cover of *Steppenwolf*, so I began a poem rather than a novel.) I had written poems before, but they were little skinny things. This was a big one. It was fat. It was dense. It could jump like a sailfish and dive like a sperm whale. It was going to be a world record.

Now there is more on the theme of coincidence. Sally and Thad and I had gone to school together. And also Diane and David. Good lord, now that I think of it, I had known Harold, too. He was a composer in those ur-schooldays. It's just that there were different connections. I think it was Sally and David who were a pair in the earliest days. Later, whenever I visited the city, I stayed with Sally, who was also a flutist. Her friends became my friends. Their enthusiasms became mine.

When I waddled, quacking softly, into the household of my friend Sally, at the very beginning of the guru-summer, and discovered that several of her closest circle were involved in a mysterious Islamic religious organization, my fate was sealed. I was certain I had conjured it all with the magic of my poem. I took up Sambilan eagerly, waiting outside the doorway in the hall above the dirty-book store where they conducted their activities. Men and women in separate rooms, strange sounds, singing and grunting—who was to say what else? It was my task to wait outside until I was called. Until I was deemed ready. It might be months. Twice a week I sat in a chair in the grim hallway while my friends went inside and did the Dalawa, the wonderful and mysterious religious exercise of Sambilan. I had barely begun my waiting period when the time came for Anna and me to move on to the festival in Wisconsin. And my poem was filled with speculation about Sambilan. I stuffed the poem like a turkey with the strophes and cadences of waiting. You know. "Anticipation is making me wait." Oh, I suppose it was better than that. At least, a little. Outside, I was serene, positively spiritual. Inside, I was like a kid on Christmas Eve.

I had planned a quiet week of serious practicing before the festival began, but Anna and I ended up spending that first week wandering in the woods and meadows around our cottage, catching frogs and snakes. Anna drew and I went through the motions of playing the flute under the rustling birch and pine trees while invisible insects sent piercing threads of sound into the warm afternoon air. These were not the motorcycle-gang katydids of the South. These were artists, performing some precise operation above us, making arcane connections through the air. And to prevent us from understanding their purpose, they made us drowsy. Finally, I took to drawing and Anna to playing one of the little bamboo flutes I had made for her. This finally seemed appropriate. We were more pure without the burden of our accumulated skills. The earth was stretched thin over glacial detritus and covered with odd mounds. We climbed the mounds and wandered among the trees like ants. The sun shone on us with peculiar intensity. Dozens of little leopard frogs leapt around us with careless abandon. Everything else was fixed, preordained, heavy with purpose. And the frogs, with all their free will, were caught and eaten by snakes. The warm afternoons subsumed into evenings precocious with meaning. Bats tumbled above us, collided with giant moths and showered us with brightly colored dust. We waited.

"Hey Jimmy, Anna! What a butt buster!"
This is Sally, toiling up the hill to our cottage. Our quiet week is up. Rehearsals begin tomorrow. I got this gig for Sally and Thad before I lost credibility with the conductor. Sally's going to be the second flutist, and Thad plays bassoon. Sally has taken to wearing granny bonnets. She looks a little like the girl on the Dutch Cleanser label. Thad has a kind of crazed Amish air about him. His whiskers grow out well past the limits of rebellion, but there they have been trimmed neatly. Perhaps it is the Civil War I see in Thad. Something, anyway, that is completed, behind the covers of old albums, something dim and out of place. Thad soon will specialize in playing French bassoon. An awkward decision. An unpopular instrument in America. Different fingerings, different sound. And he will not move to France. Now Thad is telling me something about acid stools. Sally and I begin our shit routine. Must we hear this?
". . . Great foaming event. Much less suitable than those firm, brown, compact feces."
"Yes, but what of the sliding footmark, like the first fossilized step of prehistoric man, in Great Dane poop on a Sunday sidewalk. And behind it the imprint of the behind descended. What an adventure! The archaeologist of doo-doo must . . ."
Anna tolerates this foolery well. She leads us into our little cabin and brings us tea which we sip on the screened-in porch. Sally is a bit plump with clear blue eyes. She does seem to sleep around somewhat. It is inexplicable to me. Thad is devoted to her. It is inexplicable to me because I do not find her attractive. Not because of Thad's devotion. In this respect, Thad is merely a cuckold, another jerk. But he and Sally have some magical equi-

librium. In a few years they will switch spouses with another married pair of musicians, all members of the same woodwind quintet. I will think this scandalous and amusing, already having conveniently forgotten some of the other goings-on in the big house before Mrs. Surgeon General prized us out into the world. Anna is dark and pretty, but with a nose I would wish to be just a little different. At times it seems wrong to me. I cannot decide how I would like it to be. It seems to change from day to day. Anna's sensuality is extraordinary. She understands my body better than I understand hers. But I am full of juices and energy of the dark and light sort. I do not aspire to celibacy. Sometimes, however, I forget for too long a time that I am a sexual creature, and Anna plays upon my body and lets out its devils. She is guiding me through this passage of my life. When I am admitted to the Dalawa I will pass its energies on to her in the manner of husband and wife. This much I have been told. Anna will disappear from my life in the years ahead, but she will live on in its mythology.

———————

It was the night of the first concert that Anna found the guru. What a nose (that nose again) for the world's unique children she had! This fellow, then, called himself Michael. He was dressed in cowboy boots, jeans, and some kind of Peruvian blanket, not really a standout costume for the audience, even in Wisconsin. While I was on stage, becoming intimate with a group of near-total strangers, thanks to Herr Mozart, Anna was inviting the enigmatic Michael to join us for a post-concert beer. You don't have to like them, those musicians sitting in rows around you, huffing and puffing, bowing and scratching. I have made wonderful music, as inflaming and satisfying as sex, with people I despise—but then, I suppose, the whole thing could be argued the other way around. In any event, these particular musicians were not despicable, merely unknown to me. The wonderful thing about making music is that it is not necessary, in fact, it is positively dangerous, for the musicians to speak to each other. Oh, I know some do, most do, and that I am a crackpot, but this is my opinion. I was offering it to Michael. I was taking time to sip my third beer (the first two I had inhaled), and my opinion came out, as opinions often do, with a certain amount of arm waving and table whacking.

"Yes, I like Ives, but I have read what he has to say on the subject of his music. His primary interest was to shock the old ladies, his term for most concertgoers. The man was bored, he had nothing to do. Not enough television."

"But what do you think, Anna?" This is Michael, who has had only one beer and is obviously amusing himself with my post-concert energy.

"Oh, James played in a new music group for a season, just after we met. All he would talk about when he called me was Mozart."

Mozart could have written this scene. James will continue on that very subject. The genius and invention of Mozart. Especially the piano concerti.

We might even imagine that this is a trio. And that the music flows around and through it like a river, a river in flood with various objects floating in the current. They appear and disappear as they are moved by invisible forces below the impenetrable surface of the flood. Michael and Anna speak of other things.

"It was a nice place, but very cold. I spent a few weeks there with James after he had decided to leave the job. James is very good at leaving jobs. I would spend whole days in the art museum while James was in rehearsals. It was wonderful. Then I'd come home and draw while he ranted."

James is, of course, ranting, walking to the refrigerator, tossing his beer can in the trash, and at the same time, telling a story about a composition he was forced to perform which involved at its climax the throwing of paper airplanes.

"These are your drawings, then." (Anna's sketches are pinned all about the walls.) "They're really quite wonderful." Anna smiles modestly while James seems to have veered onto the subject of multiphonics. "I'm doing some drawing myself this summer. I wonder if you'd consider posing for me?"

"There's really not a lot to do here. It might be fun."

"So you see what I mean?" I paused, and Michael and Anna looked at me, I should say, distractedly.

This was when Michael turned to me. Think of it as a key change (probably to the minor) or a new tempo.

"Anna tells me you are a poet, that you're working on a long poem."

Do I say yes and clam up? Or do I start in? There's absolutely no in-between. I know I'm foolish about the poem I'm writing. I just try to avoid acknowledging it as much as possible. However, I did not feel cautious that evening. I had some vague sense that no one had been paying me any attention, and that was enough to do in the little caution I might have had.

"I'm trying to write a poem on the subject of enlightenment. I want to write my way, little by little, into the presence of the truth. I imagine that it will be a kind of process that fits into the pattern of . . ."

"It won't work." (Here now is the central flaw in my memory. As often as I replay this scene, I cannot discover why I did not choose to argue with Michael, why I chose instead the opposite.)

In my eyes Michael was transformed. He gazed at me patiently with a steady eye and the kind of smile that was neither inviting nor infuriating.

We can imagine that the music which contained and swarmed around our separateness has stopped now. That the cabin is quiet. The chairs and table have grown a bit smaller, and the light is now odd, as if the night outside is pressing on it somehow, making its color, once a kind of lemon yellow, fade toward the pumpkin shades. We are all suddenly aware of fatigue, sleep. The way days, all things, end.

"Why not? Why won't it work?"

"Because the truth is already there. Because you are making a choice, and when a choice is made, it will be the wrong choice. What is the difference between one and two? No, no, think again."

I sat in the silence a while before I began again. Anna was sitting across the room next to Michael. We formed an acute triangle with me at the distant point. I felt as if the long sides of the triangle were wedged in the soft tender places between my ribs. I began to defend my poem. I explained that ideally, all knowledge was passed on, in the way music was taught, from teacher to student. But that in this instance, while I recognized that I was a student, I was forced to discover the knowledge myself, because there was no teacher. No one enlightened.

"But I am," Michael said.

"You are?" I said incautiously. There was more silence and I felt Anna's hand on my shoulder.

"I'm working as a fishing guide at the camp on Green River. I have a cabin there and most of my time free. Why don't you and Anna come up and visit me? We can talk more then."

Michael rose and departed. Anna bussed the beer cans. Then we two, James and Anna, went for a walk in the night, and it was now totally dark, filled with the scent of pine and the distant and cautious scraping of our feet on the ground beneath us. After a while, we came out into the open, and there were stars. Anna and I held hands and walked along the road. Neither of us said anything. After we had walked our fill and passed back up the dark path to the cottage, and after we had fallen into that same river, that once was music, but now was sleep, the Perseid meteors streamed through the sky above us. Like sand thrown by a child at the beach, showers of sparks smudged the sky above us, but we were not restless. I can see us sleeping there in the dark. We are young, and I see us as if I were a father watching his sleeping children.

We did visit Michael at his cabin the next day. It was a gingerbread house of a cabin with clover growing in pots at the door and the skull of a porcupine, all arranged artistically with driftwood. It was on the shores of a little river which was so shallow it might have splashed out of its banks, had there been a fish to disturb it. The cabin's walls were decorated with squiggly drawings which looked to me like blue bedsprings, but which, according to Michael, were the designs for monumental sculpture. He and Anna got on famously, and near twilight he took us out on the river. I had brought my flute with the notion that I could also explore the hidden reaches of enlightenment with my music. Michael said no, but I played anyway. I had in mind to play Bach, but my memory failed and I began to improvise. Suddenly the air was filled with swallows, singing and diving, giving of such ecstasy that I stopped and stared in wonder. It did seem to me then that I had called up a miracle. Of course, the swallows always come at that time of day, but it was a fine time. I think of it often. The water was calm as glass, and what was invisible in the air, disguised as supper for swallows, was supper for my soul as well. I see now that when I took down my flute and looked up at those scribbles of God above me, I was as close to my goal as I would ever be. But I could not have known, should not have known such a thing.

We told Sally and Thad about Michael, and soon Sally became his prize disciple. I was busier with the music making than she. I had a difficult concerto to play, one I had relentlessly pestered the conductor to program. I did not follow Anna's activities closely, but I supposed she was now and again a guest of Michael's. I had to practice extra hours at the rehearsal hall. I was, in those days, if nothing else, a hard worker. I could dream while I practiced.

Diane is calling me now. I don't know how she suspects that I am about, here in the pantry, "lurking off," as we call it. Perhaps Sally is not as okay as first advertised. Yes, I have been getting it on with Diane a bit, but it's really been a musical assignment. We have been preparing a recital together, and communication seemed the watchword. Anna's been too busy for me anyway, distracted by her work, which lately has been welding, a pursuit which does not seem to encourage clean fingernails, among other things. A bit of fun with Diane often leads to bruises—she is such a skinny character, and, as I may have indicated before, probably nuclear powered. I'll pretend I don't hear her.

When the festival came to an end, Michael invited us to spend some time with him at Green River. Actually, he invited Sally and Thad. Anna and I were a kind of afterthought. But Michael seemed sincere. There would be only a short delay before returning to the city. Anna and I had already decided we were going to move into the big house with Sally, Thad, and the others.

Michael did not prove to be the teacher I had hoped for. I have been put in my place time and time again by musicians—teachers and conductors—humiliated, yelled at, brought to and beyond the verge of tears; and consequently, I was sure I knew how the master of enlightenment should behave. This one ignored me and spent much time in a locked cabin with Sally. Still, I managed to barge in upon them once and discovered Sally performing a service which seemed to me considerably beyond the devotional. A teacher myself, I had always resisted certain students who seemed often to rub their softer parts against me, perhaps by accident, perhaps not. I felt I was in danger of losing my authority, not realizing in my innocence what else I might have risked.

I took the high road with Michael and Sally. I used my best material, the voice of quiet disillusionment as opposed to the impassioned rant (which everyone had learned to ignore, anyway).

"What about Thad?" I asked. Thad had gone back to Philadelphia to deal with the lease on the big house. This forced Sally to go to her best material—which was copious tears. Good defense always beats good offense.

We stayed a few more days by the side of the river enjoying the peaceful weather, but the sight of so many snakes gagging down leopard frogs, which, as I mentioned before, had reached epidemic proportion that summer, was tiring. I had already worked all the snake symbolism into my poem that I could manage. It seemed time to return to the city.

It was our last day, and I was lazing on the boat dock. I had given up practicing. Even the poem had been neglected for the past few days. The midday drilling of the cicadas had finally severed all the functional connections in my brain. I noticed that Michael was sitting beside me.

"What are you going to do this winter?" I asked. For the first time it occurred to me that Michael must have a life apart from this place.

"I don't really know. I thought I might come to Philadelphia."

Noticing my expression, Michael went on, "You know, I didn't say I had any answers for *you*. I just suggested you come up and talk. When you told me about this Sambilan thing, it was clear enough."

"What was clear enough?"

"That you need to sit outside of doors for a while."

I heard a yip. A garter snake had another frog and was stretching its head around it in convulsive movements. After crying out, the frog seemed patient, no longer struggling. The snake had no expression whatever. It was more than disgusting. I got up and went back to the cabin to pack.

The car broke down twice on the way back to Philadelphia. Once in Milwaukee, and once beside a cornfield. I threw rocks and listened to meadowlarks in the cornfield, read fan-belt magazines in the filling station. Milwaukee cost a whole weekend in the Bolivar Motel, where Anna and I enjoyed the vibrating bed. But we ran out of quarters before we ran out of Milwaukee.

Then the summer was really over, and we were moved into the big house. Anna dived into her welding projects. Sally and Thad disappeared into their room with a hot plate. Diane and I began rehearsing for a recital at the Art Alliance. We were doing two of Harold's pieces, which were so difficult, parts had to be rewritten. Much time was spent in the basement kitchen at a large round table, drinking and arguing over the music. Next to the round table a restaurant stove loomed, impressive as a locomotive, sheltering a quorum of our several cats under its mighty bulk. There was a wine cellar, a library, a formal dining room, all unused. Anna had taken over a little room on the fourth floor for painting and drawing which had tiny drawers from floor to ceiling, perhaps once a pharmacy.

Diane's piano was on the first floor, directly above our favorite gathering place, and it was there, around the big table, that Diane, Harold, Anna, and I found ourselves the night of the worldwide Dalawa. All around the world, we were told, members of Sambilan were doing the Dalawa in a coordinated effort to bring about peace and ecstasy. Diane and I had been planning to rehearse, but I had brought a bottle of vodka to the kitchen. It was my opinion that I was not achieving the proper abandon in my music making. The vodka was intended to warm me to the task. As it turned out, however, the interval in the spectrum of inebriation in which abandoned music might have been made was not lengthy, and was passed over without our notice.

Our elbows were on the table. Our voices were loud. Harold and Diane, inexplicably, had begun to drift away from Sambilan, letting weeks go by without attending; but tonight, everyone was joking and wondering about the results of the combined Dalawa. I had grown bored of my hallway vigil. It was beginning to remind me of the tedium of the Elm Street Methodist Church which had tortured my childhood. But I still longed to see and hear firsthand the source of those strange sounds. This night we were all drunk except for Anna, who tended to soak up the collective atmosphere and behave correspondingly, so I might as well say we were all drunk. Even the cats under the stove were behaving in an unseemly manner, growling and yodeling in that erotic and not entirely unmusical standoff cats call foreplay. Then Harold and Anna announced their intention to do violence to the only television set in the house, the one in the room Anna and I shared. I suspected something suspicious in their intentions and made to follow them, but Diane, always imaginative, grabbed my legs from under the table. I was profoundly and increasingly distracted until we were interrupted by a crash outside the kitchen door. This proved to be the television set, more than likely not a suicide. Diane and I, somewhat disheveled, set out to climb the stairs, but I was behind her, and became so involved with the allure of a woman climbing stairs that we became distracted again; this time, unfortunately, in a more public place than under the kitchen table.

We were discovered in flagrante. Above us loomed Thad and David, and while Thad was grimly silent, David began to howl at Diane and me. Even in my drunken state, I was ashamed. David stormed past us down to the kitchen and there began breaking objects, plates and glasses for the most part. I believe we followed him. I am not precisely clear of things at this point. I do remember that David had been soaking psyllium seeds for weeks in an enormous glass jar in one of his more obscure agrarian experiments. He had managed to heave this against a wall, where it exploded grandly, and the psyllium slime crept down the wall like a creature from a fifties horror movie. Then I recall Diane, barebreasted and weeping, sweeping up the mess while David sulked quietly. I believe I was led away from the scene of the disaster by Harold and Anna, who seemed, inexplicably, not to have had harsh feelings toward me.

Our household did not fully recover from that evening. Sally and Thad remained in regal seclusion, preferring, as always, hot plates to humanity. I spent more time working on my poem in the third-floor back bedroom overlooking the alley, where, once a week, trashpickers in late-model station wagons foraged for our neighbors' cast-off but high-quality goods. The kitchen was, I think, a more solemn place. At least Harold reported this to be the case. Anna began to spend more time with her welding teacher, Harry, who also took students in other subjects. Anna taped his advertisement inside our medicine cabinet.

> The way is not a difficult one.
> Only your lack of desire for truth keeps you from it.
> There is but one path.
> All others lead to confusion, conflict, and insanity.
> Put an end to unreality.
> Destroy good and bad,
> Right and wrong,
> Ugly and beautiful,
> Great and inferior,
> All value, moral, and ethical judgments,
> In time your entire being will be at one with reality.
> The need will no longer exist
> To differentiate between this and that.
> You gave birth to insecurity by affirming unreality
> By giving substance to values, morals, and ethics.
> There is no good or bad in reality,
> So refuse to take part in its usage.
> Follow this path and you walk in absolute peace,
> The seeds of confusion, conflict, prejudice, and insanity
> Having been destroyed.
> This is the way of Zen.
> ZEN
> WA5-6663

I remember a partial tear on the pocket fold between "wrong" and "beautiful." Here was another teacher for me to consider, but I was too deeply committed to Sambilan. The time had come for my opening. I was finally allowed into the darkened room. We emptied our pockets of change and loose objects, removed our shoes, and stood in a circle. The Helper said, "Begin." And slowly, from all around me, the men began to move, to mumble, to croak and sing. From the next room I could hear the women's ethereal singing. The awakening of male spirituality, apparently, is farther from the heavens. They were like wind-up toys, those men, some wedging themselves in corners, some circling aimlessly. I had seen similar things in the locked wards of the Missouri State Hospital No. 1, when, as a graduating high-school senior, I attempted to earn money for college by pushing food and garbage carts through sewer-like tunnels connecting the hospital buildings. Waiting for the Dalawa to descend upon me, I stood rooted. An hour passed. Nothing. The Helper told me that I must continue waiting, just as I had outside the door. Now I was to wait inside while the Dalawa moved around me like a grotesque parody of the swallows at Green River. Some evenings Diane and Harold came with me. Sometimes even David, who seemed, after the night of the worldwide Dalawa, more in need of forgiveness than even I. But most of the time I went alone. Nothing happened. I would leave my offering of a few dollars, trudge down the stairs, and walk the cold blocks home through dark litter-strewn streets. At home Anna would serve me tea and aspirin. I would have turned to Harry the welder, but he and a friend had by this time stolen the necessary tires for their ancient truck and left for Idaho.

It was not long after Harry and George left the city that Michael appeared among us once again. He seemed smaller, more ordinary, in the familiar spaces of the big house; and, oddly, he did not disappear into Sally and Thad's retreat. He remained in the kitchen talking with Harold. After a few days of camping in one of our empty fourth-floor rooms, Michael rented an apartment near the river. But every day, he could be found drinking coffee at the big table in the kitchen, trying, it seemed to me, to bring us all back into community. One morning I discovered him there alone. The smell of Diane's early-morning breakfast, a grilled slab of liver, was still strong. I suppose I was grimacing as I poured my coffee.

"You can't always live on air," Michael said. It might have been the first time he had spoken to me since he had come to Philadelphia.

I sat for a while with my cup in both hands, feeling its warmth. I had almost forgotten that a conversation was hanging. The sound of Michael's voice had died away, and I was hearing something else when I got up.

"You can always try." I met Harold coming down the stairs, and for a moment he seemed to think I was talking to him, but I walked past him.

I came up to the hallway and looked out the etched glass of the front door. The street and the house were quiet. I heard faint laughter from the kitchen. Harold's voice. I walked back through the butler's pantry toward the back staircase. I stopped for a moment in the darkness of the pantry. I thought I had seen a glint from the panel of room indicators on the wall. Then I realized that what I thought I had seen I had felt. A kind of movement inside my lower spine like a bubble rising, which burst when it reached my rib cage. Not a real bubble, not something liquid poking around my liver and spleen. Something more like the light reflected from a bubble. A ridiculous thought occurred to me. "I knew in a moment it must be Saint Nick." I think I may have said it. Then it was even more quiet, and I realized that I had found the Dalawa. In the darkness of the pantry I danced with the bubbles until they were all gone and I was filled with light. It was wonderful. Perhaps it was just an old stoned flash. An undigested mushroom. Perhaps not.

I went upstairs to the window seat above the ailanthus-studded alley and began reading my poem. It seemed to me then to be a fine thing, a piece of honest work. I had never realized how funny it was, and Anna surprised me laughing. I persuaded her to make love and we were both aware that the Dalawa had brought a change. Anna seemed pleased, then thoughtful, then pleased again. She left me in the lazy late afternoon to go back to her welding. I, for my part, did not leave my place above the alleyway until it was too dark to see.

We have all made peace with our eviction in various degrees and each after his own fashion. Thad, who found this house, has found another for his burgeoning family. He and Sally will continue to play woodwind quintets with that same French-horn player whose enthusiastic warmups so efficiently reached the ears of Mrs. Surgeon General. Diane and David have plans to leave the country. A situation both distinguished and well-paying. I am always forgetting that Diane has a foot in the other world. Harold is moving in with Michael, who has finally given up on becoming the shepherd of this little flock. Anna has in mind for us to move into Harry's old studio, and while the place appalls me, I suppose I can roll up my sleeves and clean and paint. I did it in this place. It is, after all, merely a matter of degree. You learn a difficult piece of music a measure at a time.

There are little brass pointers which are supposed to turn upward when a floor button is pressed in the dining room or in the master bedroom. The thing doesn't work. The elevator between the library and the basement doesn't work either. The wine cellar is empty and the stairs creak. Soon it will all be someone else's problem. I stand here in the dark watching the butler box, as I call it, hoping for a signal. The Dalawa, however, has been stingy, refusing to visit me again, either here or above the dirty-book store. It seems that I shall have to come out and join the fuss over Sally. It is the vacuum cleaner, which has popped open and spread its loathsome insides about, which has upset her, not any concern over her guru-child. I'll come out and the world will go on, and I will go on with it. Anna and I have much more in store for ourselves, and while I know what it is—what it was, and can only think of it all sadly, my heart still quickens when I return in this way to the darkness of the butler's pantry and wait for the bubbles to rise. Because they know me. They know where I am, then and now. And they could find me if they chose.

The Bagpipe

Philadelphia, 1972

I never thought I could live in such a place. The streets were strewn with garbage and there always seemed to be mangy black dogs slinking along the alley wall. They were generic, those dogs, flea-bitten mongrels, but to us they personified the neighborhood, lost and miserable, scraping their toenails through excrement and coffee grounds. We called them South Street dogs.

I was trying to make a living as a musician in Philadelphia, and we were living in Anna's studio. We had moved to it when the owners of the last house we lived in, a fine large brownstone in Center City, decided that we were part of a hippie commune dedicated to the devil, unwholesome noise, and bringing down property values. Anna was a potter, but she also did large abstract expressionist paintings. I stretched the canvases for her. I rolled in the tanks of acetylene so she could weld weathervanes and grotesque, impractical birdcages. I hauled sheets of lead and walnut logs for her other projects. Anna sold most of her things in a candleshop nearby. This new neighborhood was Mecca for Anna, and her studio was a logical extension of it. Where else could you work at the wheel all afternoon with clay flying and splashing in every direction and have the place look no worse afterward?

The little houses (perhaps a dozen, six back to back) were part of a single ancient building which sagged with its end to the street. Two narrow alleys gave access to the doorways and divided the structure from its neighbors, a furniture warehouse and an abandoned organ factory. The houses must have been built for poor factory workers, they were so tiny. Father, Son, and Holy Ghost. Each story a single room, low ceiled and squalid, with a steep spiral staircase. Oh yes, and a dirt-floored basement for the devil. The windows on the front walls looked out on the alleyways—on our side, the alley was less than four feet wide, and its other side was bounded by the brick wall, three stories high, of the old organ factory. So there was no light for the windows. The organ factory was empty, boarded up. Many of the houses were boarded up in the neighborhood. It's no wonder the rent was thirty dollars a month.

Thirty dollars was about all we could afford then. I had held a good orchestra job a few years before in another city—"good" meaning it paid a decent salary, but I wanted more—the city was too small, the orchestra did not play interesting music—I quit that job, moved to Philadelphia, and then discovered that a better job was difficult, if not impossible, to find. So I had been reduced to teaching, to trying to get enough freelance work to move back up in the musical world. Every time I looked around myself, I was reminded of my lack of patience, my foolishness.

When Anna and I first shoveled debris out of the house, there were dozens of corpses of kittens and cats in varying stages of decomposition. I suggested a cat-nova in the extreme past, the bodies of cats exploding in all directions, but Anna explained that an eccentric old sailor named Lars had lived there with uncountable cats. He was a neighborhood legend. He had been evicted, but still could be seen occasionally sitting on a corner stoop of the organ factory, crooning to a three-legged cat named Lizzie. We filled a borrowed wheelbarrow with much garbage, cat-food cans, the bodies of Lizzie's unsuccessful progeny, and what was probably excrement of other than feline origin. We painted, scrubbed, cleaned. But the place always smelled of cat urine, that most basic and powerful of all the elements, the distillation of misery and gloom. And it was a sad place, a place the sun never touched, the bricks bleeding rust and crumbling pieces of themselves.

Then there was Tommy. His house was next door, nearer the street. He could nearly always be found leaning out his first-story window, mumbling. It was seamless. Occasionally a few distinct words would surface from the generally unintelligible background, words like "honkie" and "motherfucker," but they would disappear in a vehement splash of foam, leaving the listener uncertain, confused. Only when the welfare checks came in was there a variation in this rich sibilant bubbling. Tommy would sing for a few hours. His favorite song was "Jesus Never Fails," a descending major sixth on "Jesus," and after returning to the original pitch, a quick upward minor second on "never," and a descending minor third to linger on "fails." In time Tommy's voice would grow more impassioned, but the song, suffering some ironic reciprocity, would become "Jesus . . . never . . . ," and again and again, "Jesus . . . never . . ." Then he and Elsie would fight, sometimes violently, and finally lapse into silence. But before long, he would be leaning out the window, particles of saliva arching down into the alley, glistening against the dull bricks, his words providing an obscene libretto for something like the opening of the dawn scene of Ravel's *Daphnis and Chloe*. I was afraid of Tommy, but Tommy never seemed to notice me. I might have been another one of those slinking dogs, if not Tommy's brother in misery, a part of the scenery, more graffiti.

One winter evening, at about ten o'clock, there was a startlingly loud knock at our door. It was Tommy, and there was a young black man behind him. When I opened the door cautiously, Tommy turned his back to the lighted doorway and spoke to the man in the shadowy alleyway.

"This is my man James. He is a fine and famous musician and he smokes good shit." Then, without speaking to me, or introducing me to the man in the darkness, Tommy walked into his doorway (which shared the same stoop) and disappeared.

"I'm Charles," the young man said, moving into the light, his voice smooth and professional. "May I come in?"

"Sure," I said. I had always lectured Anna about not letting strangers into the house, but Tommy's flattery had confused me. Charles struggled in the door with a large instrument case, something big enough for a bass clarinet or a bassoon. Anna had come down the spiral staircase and sat with an eyebrow raised. I could not tell whether this was her reaction to the instrument case or to my unexpected hospitality. Anna's perch on the staircase was at eye level, almost throne-like, but made necessary by the restricted floor space in the little kitchen.

"This is Anna," I said, forgetting Charles's name as I stared at the thing he was placing on the kitchen table.

"My name is Charles, and look here what I have to show you," said Charles grandly to Anna, as he opened the case and revealed something which at first glance looked to me as if it belonged hanging on a bathroom door.

"Oh, I've always wanted a bagpipe," Anna said.

"Seven hundred," said Charles a bit too quickly, looking around from wall to wall as if for danger. For once in my life, I did not say the first thing that came to mind. After only a slightly awkward pause, I heard myself saying, "Would you like a beer?"

As Charles wrapped his long fingers around and gazed disdainfully at a bottle of Rolling Rock, I couldn't help thinking that his hands looked much more like a musician's than my own. My hands have knobby knuckles and wide palms. Charles's hands were long and graceful, and he kept them on the table, as if for me to admire.

"It's a jazz bagpipe," Charles explained. "The best kind, perfectly in tune. It belongs to a friend of mine. He needs the cash."

He took a languid drink and finished the pony.

"You know Eric Dolphy, man? No? You should."

"He's a jazz musician," Anna said. "Roger plays jazz records at the candle shop. Another one I like is . . . Cole . . . John Coltrane. That's it."

"Yes, that's it. Trane. The main man. Now Eric plays real jazz flute. He makes a flute sing like a blackbird, you know what I mean? He plays sax, he plays bass clarinet. Get it. Bass clarinet. Like in Sym-phon-y Or-ches-tra." This last performance he gave to me.

Now to Anna. "But he plays jazz. This bagpipe. It's the same thing."

I noticed Anna was smiling and nodding her head. It gave me an uncomfortable feeling.

"I haven't got that kind of money, but I could ask around where I teach. Maybe somebody in Bryn Mawr or Wilmington would be interested."

Charles looked disappointed. He closed up the bagpipe in its case with an odd flourish.

"I'll check back with you," he said at the door. Then he turned back just as I was trying to shut the door.

"Your lady is a fine-looking woman," he said softly. I watched Charles turn the corner of the alley, and shivered before I came to myself and thought to shut the door.

Anna, who often said little, said less that night, and our love-making was strange, as if we both had tuned in the same silent fantasy. Afterward, Anna cried, and only clung tightly when I asked her what was wrong. When she finally fell asleep, I lay staring at the ceiling, listening to the mice running over the hole we had patched with paper.

"James, I want to buy it," Anna said over breakfast, her eyebrows working up and down as she studied me, trying to search out my mood. Anna was dark and pretty, but her hands were red and chapped from the clay, and in those days, she nearly always wore old coveralls.

"Well, it's undoubtedly hot," I rehearsed. I didn't have a winter coat that zipped. There was a crack in my footjoint I couldn't afford to fix, and there was a lot still owed on the wheel.

"He'll take three hundred for it, and I can get that much from my mother. I really want it. I'll keep it in the studio."

(Since we had begun living in her first choice for a studio, Anna had found an even grimmer little house with its back to

Tommy's for her studio, the third floor of which had crumbled, but the second floor had an actual window with sunlight. The landlord didn't charge us any rent because we kept out the junkies.)

"Anna, why do you want a bagpipe?"

"It's . . . I don't know really. I do. It's like it has its insides on the outside, like a drawing that shows the muscles and bones under invisible skin, and then the heart and lungs."

She brightened as she began drawing a picture in the air with her hands and arms, something she always did when she was involved. "You fill it up with air, and it becomes some kind of creature. It's as if it plays the music itself. But more than that, it's that knock on the door in the night. What could be more unlikely? A bagpipe, of all things. Don't you see!"

I tried to keep my voice calm, to use my best professorial manner.

"Anna, you'd have to learn how to play it, take lessons. I can't teach you how to play a bagpipe. And we couldn't play together. Not the way we did with the bamboo flutes. That almost worked. I mean, it's the kind of instrument that was intended to frighten whole armies. If you wanted to play with me at the gallery . . . well, it wouldn't work."

Anna gave me her patient look.

"I just want it, James. You don't have to teach me anything. It doesn't have to be a problem for you." Anna had been packing her backpack with boiled eggs and her notebooks. She said nothing more, but her jaw worked silently, as if she were chewing her tongue. We left together for a day of teaching in different parts of the city. When I kissed her at the bus stop, I couldn't help noticing how dirty her fingernails were.

I was exhausted when I came home that evening, but I stopped at the little neighborhood market. Then I had to double back and walk the long way around to avoid a gang who had shaken me down for all my change a few days before.

When I was walking by the alley to the studio, I stopped. I had a strange feeling. There wasn't anybody around, not even the old bum who usually sat on a stoop and fed the cats, so I walked down the alleyway. The second story window to Anna's studio was up, and I could hear her talking. The other voice was low, hard to hear, but it was Charles. It had to be. Anna laughed, and then I didn't hear the voices anymore. I turned around and headed back to the street. I decided it was a good time to pay the rent. The rental office was only a few blocks away, and I didn't have to pass the gang. It was the kind of place where you could cash a check or pay your electric bill. A woman in an enormous beehive hairdo sat behind the scratched and dirty plexiglass and chatted with someone invisible about a restaurant fire while she filled out my receipt.

Paying the rent always made me feel better. Another month planned and conquered. When I was a kid I had felt the same way with new shoelaces. Now, with the rent receipt in my pocket, and the groceries getting heavy, there was nothing to do but go home.

I was about to let myself in when I heard it. From the studio, it was Anna playing the bagpipe. She wasn't a musician, but she had never been afraid of any instrument. As soon as she could produce a sound, she was free, making a kind of music that only she could appreciate. It is difficult for me to describe what I was hearing—I might have called it scribbles. Things like this, I felt, would somehow be less offensive to the eye than to the ear. Finally, for me, whatever it was, it was not music. My education had spoiled it for me. It was embarrassing. The bagpipe would start and stop, sometimes with great effort, sometimes incredibly abruptly. Then there were snarls and tangles of sound as if she were moving her fingers at random, like a child. It was appalling.

I realized the milk carton was leaking through the paper bag. When I put it down I noticed Anna's raku teapot was on the table and there were two cups. The feeling of exhaustion seized me again, redoubled. I went upstairs, kicked off my shoes, and lay down, thinking I would just close my eyes for a second. But it was longer, because I was awakened from a dream that had somehow incorporated it, by Anna singing from upstairs. It was one of her bubble-bath routines, French and Italian folk songs intertwined. When she came downstairs she looked rosy, almost beatific. She said that Tommy brought Charles around that afternoon, and he had agreed to let her try out the instrument. She had given him some money. She wouldn't say how much. I hadn't known she had any at all. I reflected that every woman I'd ever known, it seemed, had had a secret pile of money. It must be the only way they can deal with the risk. I was the risk, of course. I didn't feel that I was dangerous. Even in the locked ward, nobody thought of me as dangerous. Besides, all of that was behind me now. It was just that in certain moments I tended to the dramatic. I had never hurt anyone. In my opinion, the worst thing I had ever done was to shoot birds with a BB gun. I was a teenager the first time I hit a door. It was an old door and my fist had gone completely through it. I could remember exactly how it had felt, how surprised and almost pleased I had been. That evening I sat at the little table and tried to find an opening, a way I could begin to talk to Anna. I kept trying to sort it out. Was it Charles, or the money, or just being left out of things? I wanted, I was sure I wanted, to say something, but I just sat staring at the table. Then I began to feel it coming on. I stared for a long time at a slat of the table until it began to wiggle and get dark and then bright again. I began pounding the table. It was almost as if somebody else was doing it. Afterward, I could remember the look of astonishment on Anna's face. When I was done I had cut my hand, broken a chair, the table, scattered pots and pans, and lost my glasses. Anna was crying, and I could remember also, working backwards into the haze, that she had screamed, "Stop, stop!" I wrapped my hand in a paper towel, picked up a few things, and sat on the steps for a long time. When I finally went upstairs, Anna was in bed. I sat on the side of the bed, waiting for her to say something. I was ready to apologize. I was sure that Anna wanted to say that she was sorry, too. After a while, I realized that she was really sleeping. I straightened the covers over her and she burrowed a little. Then I lay down beside her as carefully as I could, and waited for my heart to grow quiet. And quiet came gradually and slowly from the distant corners of the room. Even the mice crept silently across the paper patch in the ceiling.

When I woke the next morning, Anna was gone. I guessed she had gone to her class early to load the kiln, but I had a bad feeling. The shambles downstairs glared accusingly at me, so I spent the morning tidying. It made me feel calmer. My hand was swollen, but I didn't think I had broken anything. After all, I was a veteran wall puncher. I had often bragged that I could pick out the soft bricks. This was the day I took the Paoli Local to Bryn Mawr and taught in a kind of private academy in a converted house. Its director was very Old World and quite distinguished if you didn't mind a little black shoe polish in the bald spot. For some reason, he seemed to delight in supplying me with extremely strange students. There was the cocktail waitress, who sometimes showed up straight from work in her low-cut uniform with a distressingly short skirt, who would shake violently as she tried to play her flute. Was she afraid of me? Not as much as I was of her. And the twelve-year-old child who bragged he had had seven teachers in two years. (He was soon to have an eighth.) In between, others only slightly less colorful. Perhaps there would be absences and I would be able to practice. I had a recital on the weekend.

That evening the house and the studio were dark. No Anna. I called the YWCA where she taught, but they hadn't seen her. She was gone. I tried to think where she might be. She had dozens of students who adored her, many of them respectable citizens with their own houses and cars. She was always having lunch with middle-aged ladies. I decided to call Roger and Mary at the candle shop. It was a risk, because if Roger answered, I'd be likely to find out nothing. Roger was a former drug dealer who had achieved a kind of mild autism in coping with whatever still lurked in his system, harassing his neurons. He seldom responded directly to questions, choosing rather to describe vivid scenes of violence with the enthusiasm of a Saturday-morning cartoon. He was harmless, and a prodigious worker. Mary was devoted to him. It was Mary who answered.

"Mary, I think I fouled up with Anna today. I thought she was going to teach in Germantown. Do you know where she is?"

"Oh. James. Just a minute." There was a long pause. I could hear blurs of conversation as Mary's grip over the mouthpiece of the phone loosened. "There's no way I'd let him . . ." And Roger's voice: "Oh shit, he'd never . . ." Finally she came back on. "James. I'm sorry. Roger is pouring a big batch of candles and

I've got to help. I can honestly say that Anna hasn't told me any of her plans."

I looked at a high shelf and saw that I had a little Jack Daniels left. I poured myself a drink. There was enough for another. I drank them deliberately, staring at the plants. Then I went upstairs to bed. I took off my shirt by pulling it open from the top, the way I had once seen a tailor take off a vest when I was having my audition suit altered. All but one of the buttons flew across the room. I was asleep before I could think of anything else dramatic to do.

The next morning I didn't have to teach. I considered calling the candle shop again, but it seemed clear that Anna had made up her mind, and Mary's mind as well. I tried to practice, but I could never stand the way the flute sounded in that little kitchen—I had always preferred the larger rooms at the music schools—and the music, usually a pleasure, had become impenetrable. It was Bach, a deep thicket of constant eighth notes, and I couldn't decide upon places to breathe. After a while it started to sound to me like the soundtrack for a documentary on erosion, so I quit. I picked up an old copy of a *National Geographic* and thumbed through it. There was a picture of a little girl sitting on a porch with a rocking chair and potted plants—a piece on small-town life in West Virginia. I kept turning back to the picture and staring at it. Finally I realized that the girl in the picture reminded me of Anna, and I threw the magazine down.

I decided to go out. I walked through several neighborhoods. The desolation of our own gave way to the neat, well-kept row houses of a Lithuanian neighborhood where it seemed there was always a celebration of some Church holiday going on, with firecrackers going off at every quarter. This day it was quiet, and only an old woman scrubbing her door stoop was in evidence. Then the buildings became more run-down again, half of them empty shells. I crossed a cobbled road and entered a wasted plain by the river. Tall weeds and hunks of sidewalk angling up as if there had been an earthquake. I had to crawl through a fence, and then I was alone in something that was half dump, half meadow. The weeds were dry and hard but grew sparsely enough so that I could walk through them. There were glass circles, perfect circles, the broken ends of bottles, staring at me from the dry ground. I was going to let myself think about Anna. I had lost my temper before and broken things. It was wrong, but everything was wrong. Surely Anna understood that. The two of us had been together for a long time, four or five years. Why, we were old enough to get married. I realized that I really thought about it that way. Old enough. I had asked her once, but she had said it wasn't necessary. She had said she would stay with me as long as I wanted her. I remembered her the day I taught her how to play a bamboo flute. She had puffed her cheeks like a child, and the little airy sounds she made were like gusts of wind over still water. The sound seemed at first dusty and then clear, the way the water roughened and returned to its reflections. I tried to think of why she would want to stay with me, and after considerable effort, found myself staring at the river, at the floating snags, my mind as invisible to me as the river bottom.

There was no sign of Anna for the rest of the week, and I couldn't bring myself to call anyone to ask about her. It was so quiet around the house. I'd get up and smoke a little dope and then begin practicing, thinking I would do something about finding Anna. Then it would be dark, and I would think, "Tomorrow." And the next day the same thing would happen again.

My recital was on Saturday night. I played four times a year in a little gallery on South Street for a share of the house. This one was advertised to be a solo flute recital. I was planning to play the Bach pieces I had been practicing: my own transcriptions of three of the solo works for violin, two partitas and a sonata. And I did play one. But as I arranged the carefully notated sheets of manuscript paper on the music stand, something came over me. I announced that I was going to improvise. I had no idea what I was going to do. I closed my eyes and waited. I played one note. I began it. I ended it. Sometimes gradually. Sometimes abruptly. The same pitch. In the silence between notes I began to feel that all the music I had ever played was returning to me. I let the spaces between the notes grow larger. I could feel, almost see, their shapes. I never played more than a few pitches. Beginnings and endings. Beginnings and endings. And the long intake of breath between. I had never felt more alone, yet more complete. It was glorious. I had been playing for nearly twenty minutes when I noticed that there were only a few people left. They all looked worried. I smiled, took down my instrument, and made a grand bow.

After the applause, Frank, the manager of the gallery, sidled over and started chattering. "That was wonderful, James. How did you come to decide to improvise? Do you think we should have advertised that you were going to improvise? These were Bach people, you know, the ones who were here tonight. They probably weren't the people who would have wanted to come to hear you improvise, but it *was* wonderful. I can't remember . . ."

"I'm going home now, Frank," I said.

When I ducked into my doorway, I realized that Tommy sounded bad. Very dry. I looked at the jug of Mogen David on the floor by the refrigerator and thought about Tommy. Except for the time he brought Charles to the door, Tommy had scarcely acknowledged my presence. Once he had spat in the alleyway just as I was pushing my key into the lock. It might have been on purpose; then again, Tommy might just not have seen me. I had been listening to the inside of Tommy's head for two years. I was more familiar with its workings than I was with my own. I didn't understand them, but what did I understand? I made up my mind. Taking the jug with me, I knocked loudly on Tommy's door. There was sudden silence. I waited, knocked again. The door opened slowly, part way. I could barely see Elsie's face in the gloom. She had a bandanna tied around her head. She looked at me like a snake about to strike. I held up the wine. The snake considered, tested the air, disappeared. Elsie opened the door all the way. "Tommy!" It wasn't necessary to shout. He was limping down the stairs. Their house was exactly the same as ours, except it was laid out in mirror image. The spiral stair was on the wrong side. That and the darkness made me feel dizzy. I held the jug toward Tommy. "I thought you sounded dry. I thought we could have a drink."

Tommy looked at me without speaking. His eyes were yellow. I began to notice a sour odor. It came inexorably through the background radiation of cat urine. Tommy grinned. "Woman, get us some glasses!" There was a table, larger than the one in our kitchen, wedged against the front wall. It was covered with a plastic tablecloth. The only light in the room came down the staircase. Tommy and I sat, and Elsie withdrew to the darkest corner of the room, by the gas stove, but not without her own glass. We drank. I was feeling very strange. I had smoked some mild hash before the concert, and it was calling out for the sweetness of the wine.

I said, "You know Anna, my Anna?"

Tommy mumbled something.

"Well, she's gone, she's been gone all week. She bought that damn bagpipe, and we had a fight about it, and she left. She just left."

Tommy said, "Sometimes a woman don't know what she needs."

"Shit." Elsie was not pleasant to drink with.

Tommy continued, glaring at Elsie, "Sometimes a woman needs the back of your hand. Sometimes she gets it."

Elsie made a spitting noise and went up the stairs.

Tommy filled his glass. "Sometimes you do wrong, and you are one sorry motherfucker. You know Sarah, in the last house down there? Her old man beat her every night. You ever hear her holler? Lord, that woman could yell mortar off bricks. I think he hit her just to hear her yell. Three years."

"Three years?"

"She lived here three years. Her two kids pissed in this alley for three years. Then she left him. You know why?" He looked at me with his sad, yellow eyes.

"Why?"

"She had enough. Your Anna, maybe she just had enough. Maybe she likes Charles."

I started to feel hot, but Tommy still looked sad. There was a long silence. I could hear Elsie upstairs, humming softly to herself. "Yeah, maybe you're right. Pour me some more wine, okay?" Then I heard it. I could never tune out high-pitched sounds.

"Do you hear that?"

"I don't hear nothing." Then, "But I know what you hear. You hear that white man's music. You play that white music all the time. You don't know shit."

The palms of my hands started to tingle the way they did when

I was someplace high looking down. A narrow flight of stairs, the top of a tree I had climbed when I was a child. I wanted to tell Tommy something. Something I knew and Tommy didn't. Something that would make it, everything, all right. I looked at him. The room no longer seemed dark. Whatever those yellow eyes were looking at, it was not me. And whatever it was . . . whatever it was that I was searching for, I decided, did not fit into words.

"Look, Tommy, I've got to go. You keep the wine." I struggled with the greasy doorknob for a moment before getting the right combination with the latch.

There was a different kind of smell outside. Colder. Sharper. There was something slick on the walk and my foot slid a few inches as I moved out toward the street. I scraped it off my foot as I walked, and the smell of raw garbage yielded to the stale smell of the river. Several cats moved in the shadows. My head was clear now, and I was beginning to think I hadn't heard anything.

Then I heard it again. It was a flute, certainly not a bagpipe. It had to be Anna in her studio. I walked around the corner and knocked softly on the door. There was a light. She must have known I was there, but she let me wait. I didn't knock again. Finally she opened the door and turned to thread her way through the stacked boxes to the stairway. She kept her supplies, and a lot of broken furniture and other treasures she had found on the street, in this room. I followed her upstairs. She was wearing a blue dress that I had almost forgotten. It had been my favorite. She looked different.

"I heard you play tonight," Anna said quietly. "You didn't please the crowd much."

"I heard you, too, I guess." I looked around and saw one of the large bamboo flutes I had made for her. The holes were too far apart for her fingers to cover, so she had just held it and played one note. We had played together once at the gallery, and the one note had served as a drone. I had played a Greek folk song that worked in the right key. We hadn't planned too much for what we were going to do, because I had thought it would make her nervous. The way she had played the drone note, the way she had breathed, had changed the song. It had taken on a kind of fluttering life of its own. The audience had applauded warmly. And I had never spoken to her about it.

"Why did you play that way? Practically everybody walked out. Were you stoned?"

"Yes. No. No more than usual. I don't know. It seemed like the thing to do at the time."

Anna brought me a box with some grass and a pipe. I loaded it with a pinch of our home-grown, lit it, and took a long pull. Still holding it, I looked at Anna. She came over to me and took the smoke secondhand. It was an old custom between us, the only way she ever smoked.

"I hadn't planned to come," she said. "But the day got long, and I kept thinking about what to wear. So I did it. When you started to play like that, I thought you were making fun of me, but after a while I realized you weren't. But it was funny. You should have seen Frank's face when people started slipping out. I think he decided you were never going to stop." She paused. "I've been thinking this week. It's not so much that I'm afraid of you—but somehow I think that's what you want."

"No, it isn't what I want." I started to pace around. I could hear a foghorn from the river, and next door, through the practically mortarless bricks, Elsie was yelling something at Tommy. I stopped at the door. I wanted to feel my fist going through it. Anna looked at me as if she knew what I was thinking. Then she turned away and went on in a voice so quiet I could hardly hear her.

"I wanted to go someplace where I wouldn't hear you calling."

I looked at her suddenly.

"I don't mean that. I mean inside. Anyway, that didn't work. It would take a long time, I think, before I'd stop hearing you."

She took something from the tall pot that stood under the roof leak and held it out to me. It was the first bamboo flute I had ever made for her, a small one. She had carved and burned elaborate designs between the finger holes. It had been broken in the middle like a piece of kindling. But the tough fibers of the cane still held it together.

"I did this," she said. "I broke this flute, and when I broke it I could see you watching me. What happens"—and she looked at me with a puzzled expression on her face—"is that you break one thing and somewhere else it begins to hurt. Please don't make me another one. It's important."

There was a long time when neither of us said anything. The leak in the roof had begun pattering softly into the clay pot. I looked around the room. I was going to ask her what she had done with the bagpipe, but instead I sat down in the corner opposite the wheel and lit up the little pipe. Anna sat next to me and leaned her head on my shoulder.

A little before dawn I got up and went down to the alley with its one blank sweating wall and the dark windows on the other side where people slept. And it seemed almost that I was still dreaming, but it couldn't be, because I had walked around the entire building, and now I was standing there in the cold under Tommy's silent window. It was somehow as if Anna or Charles had given me the bagpipe, and that I knew how to play it. And I began to play, and walk toward the Delaware, and cats began to follow, hundreds of cats, shoulder to shoulder with the mice and rats, coming out of basements and shadows and boarded windows, and even dogs, limping and scraping their nails; and then, although there was no bagpipe, there could not have been, and it was as still as a city ever gets, and I was standing alone, almost shivering in the alley, Tommy opened his window, leaned out, and listened.

Mrdangam

Toronto, 1973

It began one afternoon in Philadelphia when Anna's friend Sanjiv brought over the record. Anna knew Sanjiv from long before she met me, but I still can't imagine how she kept in touch with him. As far as I know she only wrote a half-dozen letters in her life. But there was something about her that caused people from her past to write or suddenly turn up. Once, shortly after we got together, a large box had come in the mail filled with the complete works of Sri Aurobindo. From Sanjiv, of course. Anna never read one of them in all the years I knew her, but she regarded them as a kind of treasure. When we moved, which was fairly often, that box of books was always first to find its place. The day the books arrived, I went through them, *The Life Divine, The Synthesis of Yoga, The Human Cycle, Savitri, On the Veda*. Spiritual philosophy, nine-syllable words, cheap paper. I found a volume of over 600 pages that was a single poem! I wondered if anyone had ever read it. Besides Sanjiv.

I was glad enough to see Sanjiv that day. Anna and I lived in a modest little house in a horrendous slum in south Philadelphia. I was a freelance flute player, and Anna taught ceramics and welding. Sanjiv was in town for some convention of mathematicians, and his great devotion to Anna seemed to include me without rancor. He was a small man, and balding. We had met him at his hotel and were walking him through a park on the way to our neighborhood. Sanjiv suddenly handed me his briefcase, bounded over a low fence, and, with the agility of a child, climbed nearly to the top of a maple tree.

"Hello down there, Anna and James. Do you remember how to climb trees?" He then began shaking the branches, bringing down a shower of water on us. Anna was delighted. I wanted to accept his challenge, but it was a small tree with limbs that looked thin and scratchy. I felt heavy and slow, but I put down Sanjiv's briefcase and began to climb the tree.

When I had reached a place in the lower branches (it was even more difficult going than I had supposed it would be), I wedged myself in, trying to conceal my hard breathing. I began trying to shake the tree a little to see if I could dampen Sanjiv's cockiness, but Anna called out to me sharply. I was already in that awkward place near anger where it is possible to do the wrong thing. So I climbed back down. Sanjiv swung himself down gracefully and beamed at me.

"You are an excellent tree-climber, James," he offered diplomatically.

Soon we had reached our little house and were drinking Anna's tea. Sanjiv told us he belonged to a warrior caste and we all laughed together. I was careful not to laugh longer than anyone else.

There was something truly strange about Anna's ear for accents. Almost immediately she was doing her version of Sanjiv, speaking with that lilt and careful pronunciation which characterizes Indian English. Sanjiv did not seem to be aware of it. And after a few minutes of the two of them going on that way, feeling like a complete jackass, I began to hear myself doing it, too.

Imagine. "Will you have some more tea, Sanjiv? Please do stay sitting while I get some for all of us." If only Angelo and Guido and the guys in the opera orchestra could have seen me.

Sanjiv said he wanted us to hear something special, so I put on the record he brought, and we listened. What we heard was astonishing. First the drone of the tambura, and with it that sense of the space in which the sound existed, the quality of the recording (not good), and the age of the whole business (well seasoned)—then something which seemed to be a kind of animal crying. Something with the infectious inner core of a loon's call, but with an intelligence, an ancient design. The pitches were bent like the stems of winter weeds, and they appeared from and disappeared like elementary particles into a kind of cosmic limbo created by the mild boiling of the drone. After a long time I realized I was listening to a flute, a bamboo flute, very large and low-pitched. We listened to the whole piece (the record said Raag Yaman), about 25 minutes. Toward the end the tabla entered, and the music became extremely rhythmic and active, but it was the opening that had captured me. I had heard some Indian music before. Ravi Shankar was in his first bloom in those days, but the jangling of the sitar was annoying to me. This was my own instrument, stripped of the metal, the keys, the nonessential. I looked at Anna. She had tears in her eyes. Sanjiv had one of those beatific expressions he specialized in.

The flutist, I learned, was a man called Pannalal Ghosh, and though I searched assiduously in the months and years after that afternoon, I was only able to find one or two other small examples of his playing. He played a bamboo flute so large, it sounded in the same range as a Western alto flute. While it was clear to me that he was a master musician, it was that low-pitched flute that haunted me. I believed that an instrument capable of such sounds was the key to the lost magic every artist searches for. It was no wonder some Indians believed there was a raga that could make the rain come. Sanjiv was going to India that summer, so I commissioned him to buy me one, and for a thousand rupees, he bought me the largest flute the flutemaker would sell. It proved to be much too small to produce the low animal calls of Pannalal Ghosh; but worse, the holes were so far apart, I could never hope to stretch my hand to cover them. It was a mystery I could not solve. I was bitterly disappointed, but I had developed a keen interest in Indian music in the meantime.

In the next year we heard from Sanjiv often. He sent more books to Anna and to me, programs of musical performances, magazine articles on Indian music. He often called Anna, and they would talk for hours. Anna spoke softly and earnestly in those conversations, and, try as I might, I could overhear little. When I asked her, she said they talked about art, and she showed me pictures of temple friezes—voluptuous naked women, whose breasts seemed to have been inflated with air, entwined with warriors and demons. I did not like the phone calls, but when Anna said we had been invited to spend the summer with Sanjiv and his family in Toronto, I was intrigued. Sanjiv had invited me to enroll along with him in a class in Indian drumming.

"Do we have to take those damn books?"

"Oh relax, James. You always get so tense when we go on a trip. Look. It's really a small box. I don't think it takes up half the room your bamboo does."

It was true. I hadn't given up on the big Indian flute. I had gone to some of the shops where window dressers buy supplies, and found large bamboo poles. I was trying to make a Pannalal Ghosh flute. By the ingenious device of covering holes with my thumbs as well as my fingers, I had already made one flute almost large enough, and I could play the alap, the slow opening, of Raag Yaman. The sound was similar, but small, weak. I had the wrong kind of bamboo. I had the kind on which you drape silk blouses behind a store window on Walnut Street.

Sanjiv lived with two sisters in an apartment complex on the north side of Toronto. You could look across the road into a brushy field inhabited by tiny darting birds, and beyond that, more fields, and beyond that, a steely sky, that even in summer held secrets of ice and gouged stone, hints of the sweeping tangle of northern lights.

Medha, the older sister, dark and portly in her sari, welcomed us. Her speech was more lilting than Sanjiv's. In no time we were a singsong nest of well-pronounced articles and complete sentences.

We had our own room at the top of the stairs, and Sanjiv won my heart by pounding at the door when I practiced my version of the Pannalal Ghosh Raag Yaman on my home-made flute.

"I thought it was he," he said. "How can you have done such a thing? It is a miracle."

I rubbed my cramping fingers and smiled modestly.

The other sister was Kalika, a dancer. She was the baby of the family, perhaps in her mid-twenties. She did not speak much English, or perhaps she did not choose to speak much English. She certainly spoke her native Gujarati with violent fluency. She and Medha would chatter in her room and on the staircase (an important social area in the house) for hours. Kalika did no housework and never came out of her room before noon. She was treated like a princess. At bedtime, Medha warmed a glass of cream for her.

Once in midsummer, I came home with questions from the drumming class.

"What are these betel leaves that Shankar keeps talking about? Do they really make you high?"

Much giggling and rapid Gujarati.

Medha: "Often the men will sit in the shade of a jack-fruit tree and chew betel. This is very relaxing. I have wondered about it myself."

"I don't suppose you can get betel leaves outside of India?"

Sanjiv: "Oh, they are not so hard to find. Many shops have betel leaves. But . . . ," here another lapse into violent Gujarati with interruptions by Medha and Kalika, and outright laughter, "—I have never chewed betel leaves. It is the kind of thing . . . something the lower classes do. Medha and Kalika think, however, that we should try it."

And try it we did. The next day. I remember us all gathered around the staircase, exclaiming that the leaves did nothing except get caught between our teeth.

Anna nudged me. Kalika sat on the step next to Sanjiv, eyes closed, head resting on his shoulder. It was touching. There was a sweetness in her face I had not seen before. For two hours we jabbered and laughed and insisted the leaves were without effect.

When our gathering finally broke up, Sanjiv took the remaining leaves to his room.

Kalika and Medha did not spend much time at domestic chores. The kitchen was a disaster, even to my eye, the sink filled with a week's dishes, the cat wandering on the table, the counters covered with flies. The only thing that outnumbered flies in the house was cat fleas. We always looked in our tea before we drank, and scanned our food carefully.

Anna and I stood in the kitchen, looking around in dismay. The rest of the household were out in the city.

"Don't you think this would be a fine time to fool around?" I whispered.

"You don't need to whisper. And it's not a fine time for anything. Look at this kitchen!"

I wandered into the dining room where I thought I'd try again.

"You know, we're in a kind of node of sexual culture. Think of the Kama Sutra, of those great temple carvings. Wouldn't you like to do it standing on one leg in Sanjiv's dining room?"

"James." Anna looked at me with what I thought was a hint of pity more than I heard in her voice. "James, these people are celibate. Let's get to work in the kitchen. This is going to take all morning."

It was not ten minutes later that Medha and Kalika came home. Medha ordered me out of the kitchen. She said it was not proper. Anna gave me a dark look and I shrugged.

The family, I decided, had had servants in India, and the girls had never done for themselves. What must their life have been like? Sanjiv once said that peacocks were useful birds because they ate snakes, that there had been cobras in his front yard. I had a picture in my mind of ruins, something out of Kipling. It was another world, that was certain. Anna said to me one night before we went to sleep that we must remember that there were things about us that would be as offensive to Sanjiv and the girls as the kitchen was to us. I went to sleep wondering, and dreamed of large insects, cat-sized, that crunched when I stumbled over them.

Our meals together were far from routine. Sanjiv spent the days at work, returning for lunch, and at an appointed time for the dinner hour. If dinner was to be at six, Sanjiv would arrive at eight. If dinner was to be at eight, he would arrive at ten. We often ate at midnight. Medha cooked vegetable curries, puri, chapathis, other delicacies I did not learn to identify. It was all vegetarian fare. Every day or so I would slip out and have a burger at a fast-food place; but in a week, after Medha took the training wheels off the hot spices, I began to crave meat less. During the morning Sanjiv and the women would take incredibly long showers; the atmosphere of sexual suppression was palpable.

After a while, Medha and Kalika were teaching Anna Indian dance. I don't remember what the dance is called, but the basic position involves turning the feet out until they form a line parallel to the shoulders, then jumping up and down. It was difficult to imagine that Medha had been a dancer, but Kalika was lithe, her hands and arms graceful. It was her eyes, her facial expressions, that were extraordinary. She seldom, no, never, made eye contact in day-to-day comings and goings. It was almost as if she were a stranger in the house. But when she first demonstrated the dance for us, she looked at me so directly, so nakedly, I felt myself blushing. I glanced at Sanjiv in hope of understanding, but he was lost in thought, contemplating his hands. Anna and Medha were exclaiming over the subtleties of the position of the hands and head, but it all seemed to me to emphasize too much slapping of bare feet on the floor, and a considerable amount of shaking of the house and dish-rattling from the kitchen. The flies were seldom disturbed. You could drop a plate and still find a fly clinging to it after it had broken into several pieces.

After dinner, Sanjiv would tell us of Sri Aurobindo, and of the great ashram in Auroville. It was his hope, after bringing his family to Canada (only his mother and a younger brother remained in India now), and seeing to their education, to retire to the Ashram, which he had actually visited. Both sisters were involved in lectures and demonstrations of Indian culture, but it was Sanjiv's position at the university, a professorship of mathematics, which was the family's main support.

When the drumming class began at the beginning of our stay, I was greatly disappointed to discover that I was to learn South Indian drumming. Pannalal Ghosh was a North Indian musician. There are many differences between the music of the North and the South, despite the similarities. I decided it was too late for me to back out. Besides, I learned that South Indian music was much more ancient, having been less influenced by invasions from the north. In South Indian music, instead of tabla, the mrdangam is used, a single, two-headed drum, shaped rather like an elongated barrel and held in the lap. The drum is made of jackwood, a wood with the specific gravity of granite, and has heads of buffalo hide. I was embarrassed to discover that the South Indians often use bamboo flutes for the melodic instrument that are no more than six inches long.

We were a large class and there were many drums. The drum-heads were old and dead-sounding, but the jackwood bodies were sure to last forever. The teacher was a tiny man, a Tamil named Shankar, so black his skin shone a silver gray in the neon light of the classroom. He was difficult to understand, and there was much to write in the notebooks. Each rhythm had to be sung in a kind of drumming solfège called solkatu. We had three-hour sessions twice a day, six days a week. We sat in circles, whacking our drums, singing: Ta din din na, kitatakadin din na, kitatakatom kitatakatari kitataka. I was good at solkatu, my tongue having been loosened by years of double tonguing on the flute. After several weeks, my hands began to feel as if they would glow in the dark. The hand-drummer eventually develops a callus over the surface of both his hands. I was still in transition. I began to become concerned whether my glowing palms and fingers would have an effect on my flute playing, which was, after all, the way in which I made my living. Anna and I attended many concerts and learned to appreciate the long elaborate mrdangam solos. They always made me think of rain—what rain would sound like to a very small creature, an insect, perhaps. I even developed a tolerance for the small flutes one always heard, although they seemed to me unbearably cheerful.

It was nearly the end of the summer, and we had completed the last session of drumming lessons. But I had persuaded the teacher to try an experiment with me. I wanted to play a Bach flute sonata and have him accompany me on the mrdangam. It was an idea which had first occurred to me during our session chewing betel leaves. We had made an appointment for eleven o'clock on a Saturday morning, a time which effectively ruled out Kalika, but Sanjiv, Medha, and Anna were to accompany me to Shankar's residence for the experiment. I had that morning buried the last of five kittens I had been trying to nurse through that terrible infestation of fleas. I can see their little swollen stomachs, crawling with armies of cat fleas, swimming like schools of tuna through delicate seas of kitten fur. The mother had been a stray, had given her gift to the household, and when they were weaned, had ungratefully thrown herself under a bus. I watched them die one by one. Even Anna would not touch them because the fleas bit her. I tramped out to the tangled field and buried the little fellow under a stone near his brothers and sisters. Then I drove my friends to the house of the drumming master. We were only a half hour late. Early, I suspected, in the great scheme of Indian time. Our first attempt at the Bach was not especially successful because the drumming was tentative. Shankar was searching for the rhythmic patterns from which the melody generated itself. I suggested that he play only in an ordinary tala of eight beats (one which fit the four/four rhythm of the Bach) and play against my rhythms. This time my hair stood on end from the beginning, and we tumbled together through the long movement like an avalanche, every falling object, every sound, every note, the concentration of pure joy. It was more than exciting, it was devastating. I should think Bach would have approved. Charles Ives certainly would have. Shankar knew somehow when the piece would end and began his mora, an elaborate rhythmic structure in three parts containing in its subdivisions smaller three-part structures, and those containing within themselves the mystical and magic threes as well. We stopped exactly together at the edge of the most spectacular silence I have ever glimpsed. I almost slid into it, never to return, but it closed up and we sat, embarrassed, in an ordinary room, ordinary people again. Had anything special happened? We had tea. Shankar's wife was an extremely young woman with a ring in her nose. I tried not to stare at her. No one spoke of it, but I felt it was a great triumph. We finished our tea and I took Anna, Sanjiv, and Medha to a lecture hall on the university campus where Sanjiv was preparing for one of his Sri Aurobindo lectures.

Then I went to the apartment, too restless and impatient to stay with them. I wandered about downstairs. It was late afternoon, and the sun made the flies in a patch of light in the kitchen shine like jewels, iridescent gold, blue, and red. I heard the dull thud of the faucet turning off as I wandered up the stairs. I believe it was an accident, that I might have wandered out into the back yard as easily. I was full of nervous energy, thinking how careless it was of us not to have taped the morning's music. But it was Kalika at the top of the stairs that I met. And it was Kalika almost clawing at me and I at her. She was not a beautiful woman, this Kalika, but she was strong, and there was a keen smell that came from her of spice and musk which made me dizzy. Her eyes belonged high above the earth, searching for hiding things. She and I did not speak, and I remember acknowledging to myself that this had been my fantasy, and that I had been wrong to wish for it.

We were on the bed and I had entered her. She rolled over on top of me and began to thrust her hips. I remember crying out, because I thought somehow I had struck something in her too deep, too secret, she was so small. She became more violent. I don't know if I cried out in fear or pain or ecstasy. I remember feeling that she was fighting me, that something had gone wrong. I wanted to push her away, I wanted to see her face, but she was clinging to me and burrowing her face into my chest. Then I knew what was wrong. I bent toward her and whispered, "Sanjiv." I had felt his presence before I saw him at the door. Kalika began crying as she pulled away from me and covered herself. For a moment the three of us stared at each other in the gloomy late light. The only sound was the buzzing of the flies. Sanjiv backed out into the hall. I scooped up my clothes, hesitated for a moment, then I passed him by, and went into the guest room. I remember feeling relieved that Anna was not there. I was sure there was still a way out.

I was hurriedly dressing when I heard Kalika's voice from the hall, rapid and shrill, and Sanjiv's, a kind of low pleading. I stood at the door, my heart pounding, trying to decide what to do, when Kalika screamed. I opened the door and ran to the top of the stairs. Sanjiv was lying almost on his back at the bottom of the stairs, his feet above his head. He clutched the banister and was levering himself up. My first thought was that the fall should have killed him. It would have me. He seemed dazed. Medha and Anna had come from the kitchen and were standing beside him. Absurdly I thought of him in the tree that time in the park. Anna kept saying to him, "Are you all right? Sanjiv, are you all right?" But Sanjiv shook his head as if to discount the question and its answer. Medha, like Sanjiv, said nothing. She stood looking up at Kalika and me at the top of the stairs. Anna seemed so large standing next to her, so awkward in her concern.

Finally Sanjiv said, "I was clumsy in my haste to climb the stairs, but I am unhurt. I should not have done what I did." He shook himself almost like an animal, climbed the stairs, and went into his room, closing the door softly.

I went downstairs and took Anna aside, saying as truthfully as I dared, "Sanjiv and Kalika were having an argument, and I can tell it is very serious."

Anna whispered, "With Kalika's temper, I wouldn't be surprised if she pushed him down the stairs."

Kalika had disappeared, and Medha, uncharacteristically, was making dish-washing noises in the kitchen. I told Anna that I was going to talk to Sanjiv. I went upstairs and stood before the door to his room. I could hear nothing. I did not want to knock on that door. I imagined myself driving, somewhere in the Midwest, the car windows open, a two-lane road with corn or wheat growing up to the roadside. I tried to imagine what it would smell like, just after a rain. But I couldn't imagine it, so I knocked softly on the door. Sanjiv seemed to have been waiting for me.

We sat on the two chairs by his desk. I had a strong impulse to jump up and start reading the titles of his books. Perhaps he read something besides Sri Aurobindo. But then he spoke, slowly, as if he were very tired.

"James, you and I have learned very much of talas and kritis and the solkatu. Even today I am learning more about the music of my own people, astounding things. There is much for us to learn, even about ourselves. Today, you and Shankar . . . I think . . . today . . . you have . . ."

He seemed not to be able to go on. I don't know what he had planned to say to me. "I'm sorry, Sanjiv," I said, finally feeling calm. I had managed, while he was struggling, to remember what a wet cornfield smelled like. "I think Anna and I should leave. The class is over. I've said good-bye to Shankar."

"Yes, yes," he said softly. And as I let myself out the door, I heard him say again, as if he had never spoken, "Yes, yes."

I lied to Anna. I told her I didn't understand what the problem was but that Sanjiv had asked us to leave. There was such gloom in the house, Medha was so silent, that leaving seemed the only thing to do. We did not see Kalika again. The next morning we loaded the car, and Sanjiv stood in front of the apartment, watching us as we drove away.

I kept thinking that it was just an accident. It *was* all an accident, of course, the kind of chance that allowed Shankar to know when the end of the Bach sonata he had never heard would come, that allowed him to play his mora so that all would end before the abyss. And so it did.

We drove past the field where the little birds twined in the weeds at dusk, where the kittens were buried under stones. Then we drove down through Detroit, and Detroit filtered us into the Midwest where the high corn rushed past us, just as I had known it would. Anna said nothing for a long time.

"You know," she said finally, "I always thought I wanted to go to India."

I was thinking just then of telling her what had really happened with Kalika, when she went on.

"It's odd that Sanjiv didn't talk to me after he fell. But then, he didn't talk to me alone the whole visit. You don't suppose that he and Kalika . . . it's so unlikely, but it would explain a lot to me. . . . Do you know, James, that three years ago Sanjiv asked me to marry him?"

I held the steering wheel with my two hands near the top. It made me feel as if I looked steady, occupied. I could remember my father driving this way, his two hands near the top of the wheel. This was the way I would wait for her to tell me about Sanjiv. We were passing through some bottom land and the corn was several shades darker. I guessed that it was my turn.

"Well, what happened?" Now that I had spoken, it seemed to me much too soon.

"I refused him. I didn't love him." She put her hand on my arm.

"I wonder if he'll keep calling me now? After a while?" We crossed another river, or it might have been the same one again. It must have been a small one, because when I tried to look down at it, all I could see was trees.

Anna almost startled me when she went on. "I think he will. When we're not in that house, we're not disturbing their lives. Didn't you feel like Gulliver?"

I suppose I should have told her then, but we began talking about how much we missed things like hamburgers and french fries, and it all just seemed to fade away, like a dream. Then I turned on the radio and there was a Schubert symphony, an early one, full of song and with a wonderful flute part. I listened greedily.

We spent two weeks with my parents in the small midwestern town where I grew up, and Anna became very ill. She developed a serious pelvic infection related to her IUD. We decided it might have been the dancing. Concerned as I was about my hands, I never played the drumming exercises again. When we returned to Philadelphia, we began to sleep apart in our two studios, unwilling or unable to continue our lives together. We had wandered to the edge of a vast, lonely space, a wilderness where we had no idea if we would ever discover each other again.

Later, much later, I met a musician traveling with a dance troupe, whose name was Shiv Kumar Punjani. He told me that Pannalal Ghosh had not been a small man. He had been almost six feet seven inches tall, and he had slit the webbing between his fingers. That is what Punjani told me.

Teaching

Philadelphia, 1974 / 1978

My schedule was only six hours, but I'd never taught so many kids before without a break. I kept looking at my watch, and I was annoyed when they were late, even more annoyed when they were early. And they were a sorry lot, picked over by the other teachers, only a few of them unspoiled beginners. Some had played the flute a year or two with no one but an overworked band director to help them; worse, some had taught themselves.

In 1791, in the foreword to his treatise on flute playing, Johann George Tromlitz described students who have not received proper instruction as likely to produce a tone "wooden, hissing, or bungling, without marrow, shrieking in the high register and practically inaudible in the low . . ." with musicianship "either sticky and droning, or lumpy and stumbling." This man had heard *my* students. He, however, had some notion of what course to take toward a remedy. I did not.

I showed my little beginners where to put their fingers, where to place the flute on their lips, and prayed they would produce a sound. I had no idea what to do if they could not. With the others, the ones who had learned wrong fingerings and had bad embouchures and faulty hand positions, I proceeded by correcting every mistake in a gradual accumulation of annoyance and impatience. Poco a poco accelerando e crescendo. The kids came in all colors and sizes—mostly girls, but there were a few boys. Their instruments were provided by the school system and as such were barely functional. While I talked and raved, some cried, some stood in stoic silence. But nobody quit. They just kept coming back week after week, by bus, by streetcar, on foot, through neighborhoods that terrified me, timidly knocking on the door when it was lesson time. If one was absent or late, I would eat my lunch, hard-boiled eggs and a peanut-butter sandwich, or lie down on the floor and take a nap.

This was disconcerting to the director of the school, Mr. Schwartz, who often peered in the window of my studio door. He was a small man, dusty and dried up, chewing an unlit cigar which probably contained more moisture than his entire body. It was his job to monitor and supervise my teaching.

"May I come in, Mr. Baxter?"
(The merest grunt from me.)
"How are you, Thomas?"
(Thomas, my four-o'clock, who is naturally taciturn, barely nods, taking his cue from me. Thomas is in the fifth grade, a little short and overweight for his age, and has been on lesson two for the past three weeks. Two white men in a small room do not seem to bring out his inner liveliness.)
"And how is Thomas doing, Mr. Baxter?"
"Thomas is learning to lift his left index finger for the E flat after F in the descending scale . . ." I begin, and the eyes of both

Thomas and Mr. Schwartz glaze over until I am forced to pause for air, and Mr. Schwartz can interject, "Fine, fine, but let's not be too exacting. Music is fun. Carry on, gentlemen."

"Mr. Baxter, my flute don't work." This is good for the rest of the lesson. A key is stuck, a spring is bent, missing, the flute has been dropped, a dog has chewed on it.

The kids like my little screwdrivers, the funny look of the metal tube when the keys have been removed, like Swiss cheese. And time only passes when I am repairing, never when I am teaching . . .

Mr. Schwartz was patient because my students were patient, and because I had been foisted on him by a musician whom he owed a favor, but he employed many other teachers who had already learned the trade. He suggested frequently that I lighten up. This seemed only to inspire me to greater fanaticism. Then, in a brilliant stroke, he suggested I take some students on recorder. I needed the money, and from his perspective, since the instrument involved would not be the almighty flute, I might be relaxed enough to absorb the rudiments of teaching.

Jodi was my first recorder student. She was a tiny thing with wispy blond hair. Her one enormous front tooth (the other was just cresting) gave her a kind of demented Bugs Bunny look.

"Do you know my father is a scientist? Well he is, and he traveled to Paris, France, and Mommy had to feed mice to Alvin."

"Is Alvin your little brother?"

"No, Alvin is an owl. Little brothers don't eat mice."

"They don't? Well, I'm sorry to hear that."

"Mommy is an artist, but she doesn't like mice. We keep them in the refrigerator sometimes. I can draw, too."

My heart sank when I discovered Jodi could only sing instead of blowing into her recorder. We spent the lesson pretending to blow out birthday candles, and toward the end, were producing less vocalization. Time passed. To my surprise.

My studio was on the second floor of the Northside Music School, and I taught there three days a week. The walls were the yellow of a dusty legal pad. A rather abstract finger of God giving life to Adam disguised as a water stain adorned the ceiling. This was the cell in which my life passed, or rather, seemed locked. When I entered that room, it seemed that I had never left it, that all things began and ended there. There was an ancient upright piano standing against one wall. The cover over its keyboard was frozen, not locked, shut. Once I managed to work it up about an inch and plunk a key. It was nearly a whole step flat. Brought up to pitch, the piano probably would have exploded. In the other wall was a window which gave me an excellent view of the parking lot which was bounded by weeds and a few straggly, smog-blighted trees. And, completing the decor, there were two Grandma Moses landscapes in cheap frames, probably cut from magazines. I used the piano for a desk to fill out my roll sheets. While my students played, I gazed out the window at the parking lot, or deeply into Grandma's fields at harvest time, absenting myself successfully until it was time to suggest, "Why don't you play that again, this time perhaps, with B flats."

Jodi was singing again at her second lesson, but we managed to learn "Mary Had a Little Lamb" with sounds produced primarily by the recorder. She was ecstatic.

"I drew a monsthter. Want to see?"

"A monsthter? Why, this looks like a cat. A nice pussy cat."

"It does not. It's a monsthter. My Mommy draws monsthters and makes a lot of money."

At this point there was a knock on the studio door.

"Come in," I shouted in a voice intended to carry over the drum set next door and penetrate the substantial, if not soundproof, studio door. After my third "Come in," thoroughly annoyed, I went to the door myself.

I was startled by the woman standing there and immediately appreciated subconsciously that she was accustomed to a startling effect, that she had probably intended it in this instance. This was Jodi's mommy. The resemblance was unmistakable. She had Jodi's shade of peach-blond hair, but it was cut so short that the shape of her face, her skull, made a single impression, and it was stunning. She was not exactly what I expected to see in the hall of the music school. The more I stared, the more interesting she seemed. I was absorbing the details of her vaguely South American attire, having completely forgotten the thunderous aggravation still echoing from my last "Come in"—having forgotten myself, amenities, all things but this amazing creature— when she said, rather as if I were invisible, "Pack up your things now, Jodi." Her voice was reedy and unperturbed. And as I began to blush and realize myself, "You, of course, are Mr. Baxter. I'm Jodi's mother. Won't you tell me how she's doing?"

I managed, I suppose, to blather a bit along the lines of what Jodi had accomplished, and she and her mother, whose name I learned was Clair, disappeared in a swirl of scent which I think may have been a man's cologne. There were children running and shouting in the hallway. The six-o'clock Handel violin concerto had begun across the hall, and Mr. Schwartz had brought me a new student, a mailman who had bought an old conical-bore wooden flute in a pawn shop. I think I told him it was as good as any.

A few weeks later, I used my flute to illustrate a passage in one of Jodi's lessons, because I had forgotten to bring my recorder. Jodi was captivated, and in spite of myself, I soon had another flute student. Unfortunately, Jodi's enthusiasm was inversely proportional to her natural musical ability. In all my years of teaching, I can recall only a few other students who were both tone-deaf and rhythmically deficient. But Jodi was smart, lively, winning, and the child of an interesting woman.

"I drew another monsthter today. Want to see?"

"What is it?"

"It's a snake. It's like the ones Mommy paints."

"I tried to paint a snake once, but it got away."

Jodi's snake was really quite impressive. Besides its original coloring, it featured a rather amazing (but perhaps accidental) play of perspective.

"You don't think Mommy paints monsthters at all, do you?"

"I do so."

"Do not. And I've already played 'Oats, Peas, Beans, and Barley.'"

"Not in this key."

"What's a key?"

And until Clair gathered up Jodi, and invited me to dinner on the weekend, I expounded unsuccessfully upon the subject of tonality, beginning, as I felt I should, with the ragas of ancient India.

Jodi's house is only a short walk from the train station. My directions have been clear, I have a little pencil map drawn on the back of a parent's practice report.

The map does not show the size of this house, however. It's Hawthorne, no . . . it's from *Wuthering Heights* but with Miss Havisham's garden. What a place. I have to climb over quarry stones and uprooted slabs of sidewalk to get to the front walk. Oh there, on the other side of the house, a driveway complete with an unwashed Peugeot. There seems to be no bell. I knock.

Jodi answers the door, seeming even smaller in the cavernous entryway, flitting about me like an errant photon.

Clair appears, wearing an apron.

"Hi. Would you like a glass of wine? Steven's still in London. I thought he might be back this weekend, but the conference has been extended. Conferences are always extended so the guys can think of cute names for elementary particles."

I am occupied with the spectacle of an enormous curving staircase, which seems to be either under construction or experiencing demolition, when Clair thrusts a wineglass into my hand.

"It's interesting, isn't it. Most of the house is like this. But there's plenty of wall space. And it was a bargain."

And on the walls that I can see are several large canvases, apparently landscapes, in colors which are a bit bright for my taste. I begin to formulate an appreciative observation when there is a racket from the front door and Jodi runs by carrying a bundle.

"Jodi's spending the night with her friends." Clair brushes my shoulder with her hand as she hurries to the door, calling instructions. I am left alone with my wineglass, which, when I finally summon the presence of mind to examine, I realized I have drained.

I should say that when I first saw Clair standing framed in the doorway of my studio at the music school, I had a kind of premonition mixed in that general bombardment of thoughts and feelings. I have had that premonition one other time and it was equally prophetic—it was a kind of sexual certainty, that I was, would be connected to the woman who sparked it in me. After each of Jodi's lessons there was another moment in the doorway, a few words exchanged, an odd little continuum, charged with longing, somehow amplified by the out-of-tune noises from the hall. Well, I suppose, it only seems to me now there was certainty in that business with Clair. I knew as little about the future then as I do now. But Clair had made up her mind. In some dim way, perhaps, I was capable of sensing this.

We finished the bottle of wine and began another. Then, after some rather restrained necking, she led me up the unfinished staircase to a large dark bedroom which smelled a little of mildew and a little of something else. Something odd and hard to get at, but still evident, like the well-water taste of ginseng at the back of your throat. Her body was warm and beautifully smooth, and it gave me so much pleasure to touch it, to rub my face along it, that she became impatient and pulled me to business. Lovemaking is a little like being in a clock. Some of the wheels are going very slowly, imperceptibly, and some of the wheels are going at breakneck speed, even reversing themselves. Everything you see is so close up it becomes an abstraction—a knee, the curve of a breast—the two shades of skin, and a thousand shades of shadow, limbs and petals. And mostly there is the sound of bodies breathing, of air being drawn into the clock and spun into feeling, then sent out into the room to watch. We were lying together in a kind of charged quiet, our bodies not finished, but waiting, hovering like the air around us, when I saw the owl. It was a barn owl with that ghost-white child face, and it was perched in the corner of the room on a kind of rustic dresser. It turned its head soundlessly and closed an eye and seemed to me to become larger and less determinate for a moment, then smaller and more focused. I thought at first I was hallucinating, but there between us was Clair, and at that moment she reached out to me, and before our fingers laced, I forgot about the owl.

———

It's earlier in the evening and I'm sitting at the kitchen table with Clair. I've been looking at the landscapes and they're unsettling. In some of them, there are tiny figures, Jodi's monsthters, but in most of them there is nothing overt. There is, however, an unreality pervading them, their trees and grass, the edges of things,—I can't describe it even now—that is powerful, amazing. I'm telling all this to Clair, and she's heard it before, but she likes to hear it. It's like her hair. I can't help thinking of the skull inside. Its shape. I have to take it in my hands. I'm usually a shy person, but I can't resist touching this woman I hardly know. Taking her head in my hands, really not expecting her to respond. I tell her I've come out of the painting and she starts kissing me and it all begins.

———

"I didn't intend for this to be quite . . ."
Clair drifted off, or her mind raced ahead, I couldn't tell which. Then she rolled over abruptly and looked at me with her chin in her hands.
"There was an attraction. I had in mind a nice fuck. But it's always so perverse . . ."
"What's perverse?"
"You know damn well what. What's between us. You're going to want to come back here, and I'm going to want you to, and Steven's coming back from London. And Jodi. And why did you say that about the painting?"
I was looking at her behind. It was all I wanted to do. But she dug her fingers, her nails, into my leg (I was sitting crosslegged on the bed) and shook it.
"Why?"
"I don't know. . . . Really. I was looking at that big landscape in the hallway. And all of a sudden it seemed so near . . . like a real

place. You know, a place to make love. And it felt like I was already going to kiss you, but I hadn't, and there was still no reason I should, we should. So I just said something on the way."

And I tried to kiss her again, because I had given myself that feeling again talking about it, but she held me off and gave a fine show of thinking hard again, so I went back to watching her behind, which was a quiet thing to do. And then I saw the owl again. It made a kind of shrug, ruffling its feathers, but there was no sound. I suppose it had been there the whole time. It seemed calm, but Clair told me later it was rather a jumpy creature. I wondered what an owl thought, sitting there in the near dark, the room fuming with sex like mist coming off a lake.

I'm back in my studio taking a little rest on the floor. The hand of God has been improved upon by last night's rain. But I must share my floor space with a bucket. Thomas has missed his streetcar again. I know this. He does not play truant. He is a slow and loyal soul. He will be here. Eventually. It has been two weeks since I heard from Clair. I visited her a few times before that, late at night, after Jodi was asleep, and, of course, when Steven was out of town. The last time I saw her I met Steven, an impossibly cheerful man, loud and plump, who really does have that plastic liner to protect his shirt pocket from his pens. There were, in fact, several people present. It was almost a party. Steven announced his admiration for Josquin Des Pres, put on a record, then proceeded to ignore it, telling loud stories which tended to depend upon resonance peaks and other arcana for their humor. Clair was as elusive as the owl. A dark woman with extremely thin, bony hands soon monopolized me with an endless list of questions on subjects which might possibly be of interest to a musician. She carried out her assignment well, exhausting me into an early exit. In one brief telephone conversation, Clair has given me to understand that on a sheet of paper with a line drawn down the middle, there is a long list of bad things, of dangers and disaster on one side, and on the other nothing but a question mark. I did not argue with her. I cannot argue with her even now, as I watch this rusty drop gather itself at the very tip of God's finger and plunk in the bucket beside me. But that question mark has a lovely curve, and the dot beneath it . . . why is there a dot beneath it? Now I notice the knocking at my door. Thomas and his dark little knuckles are at my door. Dot, dot, dot.

Jodi continued to appear at her lesson time, with occasional interruptions for flu and field trips. The school was busiest when she appeared and departed, and I did not discover her means of transportation. I had begun to abandon my old-fashioned teaching method which even contained a fingering chart for the open G-sharp system flute, an anachronism only in existence in England, where such things are treasured. We played songs like "Long, Long Ago," "Polly-Wolly-Doodle," and "Oh, Dear, What Can the Matter Be." I had moved a few inches through history, but these melodies did not spark any recognition in Jodi, or any of her confreres. Her week of practice (if that is what it was) consisted in gradually forgetting and distorting the rhythm and melody of her assignment. The more misshapen the results, the more time she had probably spent practicing.

"You know, Mr. Baxter, I'm sad."

"And why is that now?" (I had for no particular reason affected an Irish lilt.)

"Mommy won't let me see her new pictures. Well, she never does, but she says there aren't any monsthters in them. And she's going to have a show, and I get to help, but I always liked the monsthters best."

I couldn't think of anything to say, so I played the next song on the page, a Bach chorale melody titled "Christ Lay in the Bonds of Death."

"That sounds weird. I don't think I like to play the flute anymore."

"Well, I feel that way sometimes, too. Let's just skip this piece then. Maybe 'Three Blind Mice' will be more fun to play."

"Are you going to come to Mommy's show?"

The next student was in the room and Jodi was carting her

flute and music out the door into the cacophony of the hall. I was going to say, "I'll try," but I thought better of it. Anyway, she didn't seem to try to hear me. It was as if I ceased to exist beyond the discrete boundary of my studio door. So I turned my attention to my mailman, who had brought me, in lieu of a prepared lesson, a catalogue for tropical fish.

I received a notice for the show in the mail. It was to be in a small gallery close to my neighborhood that tended to specialize in pricey ceramics. I had been there a few times and it seemed to me that the place was much too small for Clair's large canvases. Thomas was not late for his next lesson, but appeared with his right arm in a cast. He told me that he had fallen off his bicycle, that his mother had turned in his flute—she had decided he wasn't making enough progress. He wanted to say good-bye.

"Good-bye, Thomas," I said, extending my hand. Thomas looked at me, smiled, and shrugged. I grabbed his left hand awkwardly and gave it a squeeze. Thomas moved slowly out the door. What did his mother think these lessons were for? I could have told her he wasn't making enough progress two years ago. He was coming to the lessons . . . I got up abruptly and tried to blink Grandma Moses's fields into focus.

The opening of Clair's show was on a Saturday. Since I had received no personal invitation, I did not attend. But Monday was a day off for me, and I decided that I would look at her paintings that afternoon. The gallery was part of a neighborhood that had once been a center for retail apparel.

Times had changed. A smoking comet or a freeway had scared out the old merchants. Only art is fearless. The gallery had deep display windows framing the entryway. Most of the remaining ceramics had been crowded there. The back half of the long room was devoted to Clair's show. I walked around rather quickly, trying to take in the whole thing. There were several large canvases I had not seen, more landscapes, but with no figures, these featuring a kind of geological underlay—a roadcut view which tended to suggest hazy buried shapes. The colors were more subdued also; light leaked rather than poured. It was almost sad, slow as Thomas. Nobody was around, and I congratulated myself. Toward the back of the gallery was a kind of half-alcove and there was a single medium-sized canvas mounted at an odd angle. The viewer was forced into a small space that could contain only one person comfortably. A little Duchamp business, I thought, and then I saw the picture. It was dark, much darker than Clair's stuff. I thought for a second as my eyes moved into it that this must be something that didn't belong in the show, but there was the face of the owl. A trompe l'oeil owl. And in the foreground, careless as a lava flow, was a woman's haunch and the corner of a bed. The owl was extraordinary. It got out of the darkness in a particularly startling way, and its odd expression seemed to illuminate the woman's naked body. The body which dissolved into that lost foreground. It was exactly what I had seen. The owl even seemed to change focus as I watched it.

I walked to the front of the gallery where the ceramic toasters with breasts and polka-dot taxicabs were gathered. That was when Clair and Jodi came in the front door. We all smiled and I felt as if I wasn't going to be able to breathe, but it passed.

Jodi walked up to me and said, "Did you know? Is that why you didn't come?"

"Know what?"

"That Alvin died. We had a funeral and everything."

"Alvin has been with us for three years." Clair rested her hands on Jodi's shoulders. "He had an accident. He must have gotten excited and hit his head against the chest of drawers or the wall."

"I'm sorry about Alvin, Jodi. I'd better get going." I was trying to read the expression on Clair's face. I thought she wanted me to clear out.

"No, please don't go." Jodi started crying.

Clair knelt down to tend to her and looked up at me.

"Couldn't you come home with us and have a little supper? It would make Jodi feel better, wouldn't it, pussycat?"

Jodi nodded in agreement while her mother dabbed at her tears.

The three of us had scrambled eggs and toast and sat together at the kitchen table. Steven was in Boston. Alvin was in the back yard. Jodi showed me the cross she had made by tying two sticks together. It was a large cross, even for a creature the size of an owl, and Jodi must have used nearly all of a ball of string to tie the sticks. The grave was in the back of the garden behind a row of dead sunflowers. Jodi held a flashlight for our trek through the weedy ruins.

"He never did much but sit in the corner. I guess he thought about stuff. He always seemed to be thinking. Did you see his picture with the naked lady? I made his picture, too. Mine's better, I think. Did you ever look at Alvin?"

"In the picture?"

"No, in Mom's bedroom."

"Well, I did see him one time. I thought he was a little scary with his big white face."

"I think he's looking at you in the picture. He looks like he's looking at you."

I felt a hand on my arm and I jumped. It was Clair, of course, and Jodi laughed. We made our way back to the house together as the wind picked up and rattled the husks and stalks slumbering around us.

Jodi asked me to tuck her in and I felt a little awkward, but she seemed so sleepy and content snuggled under her covers that I could remember keenly what it felt like to be a child at bedtime.

I stayed that night in the dark room with only a ghost of the owl and the woman who had painted herself almost in the way I saw her in our delirium. And because of the question mark, we slept little, painting each other with our fingers, our faces, and with our tears, but soon it was cold morning and I kissed her eyes, which she would not open to see me again, which she squinted shut, and I kissed her hand, which was a fist, and prepared to let myself out of the house, but I thought of Jodi, so I went to her room to see her sleeping. She was all but hidden in a great tangle of her covers, and I was disappointed, because I wanted to see something of that child-peacefulness she had shown me the night before. As I looked around her room I noticed something colorful partially covered by some papers on her little desk. I uncovered it and it was her picture of the owl. It was in fact the same composition, and really very good in that respect. The owl was big and white and scary and there was a female form in the foreground and the rest of the picture was dark.

The owl was looking out with yellow eyes, but there was one other spot of yellow in the picture. Jodi had drawn a little door in the background, and peering through it, with hair yellow as Alvin's eyes, was a little girl. I carefully put the picture back on her desk, climbed over the stones and concrete slabs in the front yard the way I had come once before, and took the train back to the city.

I heard the show was a success and that several large paintings were sold, including the one of the owl. I would have bought it myself, but it was much too expensive for me. Besides, being a musician, I'm used to remembering things that only exist in a moment and are then gone forever. I think it's an important skill of living.

Mr. Schwartz wanted me to change studios last year, but I refused. I think he's a kind man at heart, and so was willing to tolerate my attachment to this room at no little inconvenience to himself. I have, after all, become a better teacher. I even have a waiting list. But it's really necessary for me to be here. I sit in my usual place and the outside world is framed in the window, or I see the hallway through the door—a space that is sometimes so full of bustling children and even adults that I have to call out to them to be quiet, that I'm working, that *we're* working, my student and I, and we need to hear. Jodi is still among my students, and she's passed out of her graceful childhood into an almost matronly adolescence. It's an odd thing. She does not look very much like her old self. I should say her young self, I suppose. We do not speak of those old times when the pictures poured out of their frames and places became confused. Sometimes we talk about school, but mostly it is the business at hand. How breath support and good intonation go hand in hand. As Tromlitz says, the student "must think all the time about what he is doing and learning to do, and try to get things straight by pondering and reflecting on them continuously." And even when, as I sometimes do, I see another face momentarily when she tilts her head a certain way, I take comfort in those quilt-like landscapes on the wall, and in the ancient water stain above me. This room is my proper place, and it almost seems I have been here forever.

on the floor of your living room. Lucy invited me over, and it's true, I hadn't a clue that she was interested in me. But it was a hot, hot day and I looked at Lucy and couldn't believe she was just sitting there saying she wanted to do it with me. Nothing like that really happens to people. I couldn't blow it. It was just that one afternoon. I told her I was leaving the city. I suppose it might as well have never happened—as far as you're concerned, anyway. But for something that might never have happened, I think about it a lot. Tangled and sliding with Lucy on that hot, hot afternoon. Mercy. The things we have an appetite for. But that was years ago, long years. I had given you up for dead, file closed, lost, forgotten, and then, out of the blue, no, the brown, my spider-riddled mailbox, you appear, forehead of Zeus and all that, practically dripping with the waters of Lethe, a smoked salmon in your shirt pocket—and you are the same Franklin, bravo. No small feat, even for you. A coup, your settling down bucolic to write in Ireland of all places, and just down the county from old man Yeets, your bad jokes keep reminding me of themselves, I don't know why. How would anyone know that cows could do that? And if the peasants are that nasty, why camp in their pastures? You'd think that after so many years, they'd . . . but there I go. And a novel. How long does it take to write one? I'd like to write a novel about Lucy's tongue. But then, but then. Let me tell you what's happened. The sun's come up a few thousand times since I've seen you but the mornings we get, the ones when we look around and see something, or when the phone rings and it's Lucy, you know what I mean—God, you're out there right now, putting off writing a novel. And doing it well. That's a wonder. You've got to kick a lot of weeds with that weighing on your butt. Watch where you step, sailor. Anyway, it wasn't long ago I got this job. It's a wonder Hobbs knew where I was. It was a crummy audition, everybody crowded into one room, no place to practice, and I knew a lot of the people there— didn't make it easier. But it made me mad and I played louder, I guess, and they hired me. It all sucks. A bird can stand on a goddamn stick and sing and it doesn't care whether it was a quarter or an eighth rest in between. All it wants is to get laid and it doesn't even know that. Me, I'm depressed when I hear how I play, because that's supposed to be me. Actually, by the time I fingers like, like wheat or coins or kittens, you know, all the days, the nights, the goddamn years, you know about plenty of them, yourself, and she sat there like Gurdjieff's bandit, I can't go, I can't go. And until it got dark I talked and she didn't listen and it didn't occur to me then, or later, or even now while I'm saying this that I didn't have to go, that I'd been to that place before, that she had, too. But the guy that locks the gates came and locked them and we didn't notice, the fountain was turned up a little and covered us like F major in second violins and we didn't hear. So we had to go to the gate all tear-stained and like monkeys with our hands on the bars call out. Let life go on. Come and open the gate so that we may . . . what a hoot as my friend Billy (you don't know him) would say. He's a drummer and the dope he gets is righteous, shows the way through all material things, walls, chairs, stone but not stoned. Anyway, I still had a tour, you know, before it was time to leave for Nashville, and after that, when I got back, Anna had gone off to West Virginia. Isn't that where Lucy came from? Damn she was a sturdy girl, a strong girl. I should have been a farmer. I guess that's what you are now, me fine bucko. You've got to tell me what you're growing is it potatoes or corn or alfalfa or are you raising those little trucky cabbagey things with great flat waving spines and tentacles. What do you put in novels? Cows of course. And sheep. Sheep come with dogs and shepherds. Ever watch a dog out with his nose, making the shape of the Mississippi-Missouri drainage from the left-field fence all the way to second base—you're seeing Genghis Khan spread over Asia, migrations over the land bridge into North America. These are the insights my friend Billy brings when we sit among our taxonomic kin, the table legs and sticky ice-cream bowls. So, sheep, shepherds, I think I've got it, perhaps . . . no, maybe, maybe is the word . . . it rolls lower in the mouth (if you say it right), a swamp the mouth, alligators and Lucy's tongue—maybe I could make a book, fill it with fishhooks and whale buttons, guys with scars and peg legs, but your shepherds with their dim blind dog-nose dowsing rods will give you a story if you let them. So Anna's in West Virginia and I've been in the mountains of Lucca for two months sharpening my Questo trano va a Milano to a dragonfly's pecker. I'm wasted, the concerts were good, reviews incandescent like flowing lava,

What Mozart heard, for that matter. So be huffy. It was what, a dozen years ago, and it happened, or it didn't happen—life is like that. Look back in your novel. If it's there, if you're not out kicking rocks into cowpies. Where Lucinda takes Roderick and bites through his underlip . . . have her drive off the cliff in the Daimler. How's that any different? Besides, I'll bet you don't know where in the great forlorn state of West ferG or whereeverfor she now resides anyway. Hair in curlers, smoking a cigarette, watching the soaps while three mucus-trailing rugrats . . . need I say more? At least I know Anna's back in the city. Granted, she's a bag lady now, she does not write but she will listen on the phone. I call her and we sit there. She's always soaking in the tub. Metaphorical or not I couldn't say. Little voices like Ludwig's post come and go as the wind rubs the wires in South Dakota. Sometimes I ask her to come anoint my loneliness with her vivacious presence. But mostly we sit and review the rhetoric of rocks. I've met this girl (Aha you say) not a southern belle anyway. Says she used to lay her oboe teacher for reeds. I told her the idear of it made me horny but it seemed to me, a teacher as you well know, not such a good idea morals being what they are will get corrupted but it's hard to make a good reed I think she blew it. No, actually she thinks that's disgusting but she likes to fuck only (when) we fight a lot. That seems to be her preference, her what she likes. She gets me mad. It's her gift. I am not a suitable lover until I'm ready to punch holes in the wall. It's all manipulation, building nests, bright-colored ribbon, broken blue glass, here in a circle see what I've brought you I'll just fan this gravel gore this elk one moment please. Did she do it during lesson time, or later, I should ask. My own students are dangerous enough Oh professor doctor mister master please show me how to form a more perfect embouchure. Suck on something round, honey. Next. She lives with this biker on a hill and he works nights so she sneaks me in and will only do it in her/his house. There's an old guy who sneaks around also peering in windows. Part of her cast I suppose, I wonder tenor or baritone. Cats all over the place, but they make too much noise escorting the prowlers. Then we wander on the hillside disturbing other less fortunate lovers. Lower-class lovers. Level lovers. Stepping over lovers. Good donut shop down the street, same old stars from the hilltop among damp newspapers and cold condoms. She has nice eyes. Has been through it some. Put that in your book. It's wandering in the desert I'm sure about, but when you write, you have to leave out the straightaways, right. You just record the turns. I made up that stuff about Lucy. Think. Think. Put it in your novel. I could have said come away O human child and we'll take this on the road and we'd have gone to Wisconsin or someplace where big sturdy girls fit in. For old time's sake I let it be (I thought you might be coming in the door). Remember that one time. No, you were too drunk. Stay around the sport long enough you'll find yourself playing your old team. Then will the fans cheer?

J

April, 1981
Nashville, Tennessee

Dear Franklin,

I didn't tell you I suppose I bought a motorcycle and the first 5000 miles are the hardest. Somewhere I read that. It was around mile 1500 in southern Illinois and I was passing a truck passing a truck and ran out of road. Cornfields are hard to slow down in but I was doing fine until the culvert. Flushed them woodchucks and bunnies good. Got a broken collarbone and some ribs. Love them ribs. Just don't breathe for a few weeks sonny and you'll do fine. I'll just lie (lay me) around a few weeks and catch you up. Don't think I'm the biker type. Yet.

J

June, 1981
Green Spring, West Virginia

Dear Franklin,

Take the arrrr from crows and you've got cows. Look at that now. The one all pointed looking out the one eye while the other waits (the other eye, not the cow, that's yet to come). Now here they come now cows look low for lunch step in soft holes where water oozes up, piss on flat rocks like a chapter in the Bible, this of all things you should know. Chew and fart. The manufacture of methane and taking a dim view of things. Even on a bright day. Crows have a personality disorder, it's what makes them crows, like me, poets of invective. Arrrr. I'm in my convalescence. I called Anna and she came and brought me to this place. Roger's farm in West fer fucking G. Here I too could novel it up if goats and ratty chickens were my madeleine. But I'll write something because toot-not and breathe low sweet chariot, my crack medical team has strongly advised and after all we are in good leech country. Roger and Mary are Anna's friends from way back but they do not hold my character in esteem although Roger is usually high enough. Anna will not do those things she did once and I am not much up to those things mostly I did once (and hope to do again) so it is a sorry reunion but plenty of chicken soup shall heal me I am beginning to understand the language. Genius of caution I said to myself I think once or at least dreamed of these bawking interrogatives. Remember the don't-lose-your-gum jokes. Also unlike the city to eat them you've got to kill them. Roger's style is to hold the head whilst twirling the chicken in a high back swing. Far too messy says I and the chicken flies into a patch of mint and marches about like Cherubino bawking prodigiously. You must be careful wiping the blood out of your eye or you'll lose track of her. (I haven't et a rooster yet, you have to give them a most fearful bake.) Mary, sweet child, uses a chopping block and the damn thing runs off just the same. Could use a kid or two here just to chase decapitated chickens. When employing Mary's system one gets to watch the head like a ventriloquist mouthing those distant and ever diminishing bawks. Mary models for Anna who does draw fine and suggested I try the same, but Mary's skin is pink and soft and drawing is not what comes to mind and that is not where it comes to anyway. Roger is slow of foot but could I think make a chorus line out of my remaining unblemished ribs if he so chose so I draw the outlines of Mary's neat little titties and grit my teeth.

J

September, 1981
Nashville, Tennessee

Dear Franklin,

As you can see by that blurry round thing, octopus sucker mark about my stamp, I am back at work, spitting on my music, giving them better than they deserve, my bitter colleagues say as they screw up Haydn Mozart Mendelssohn Tchaikovskyrachmaninoffdebussybrahmsetc. I am much better but not all. Roger threw me out but Anna has a car and drove me safely to the bus station. It was an artistic contretemps I did it again. Anna surprisingly took up for me it was just I told Mary I wanted to draw her pee pee. Seemed like I had seen that theme in some of Anna's work. Everybody figured I was ripe for export then and I suppose. Tired to death of birds singing, chickens roosting, dogs sleeping on their backs now there's my pee pees. What a fool I was. I could be stepping in goat scat now. Which brings me to your news. No it was not I. I did not post your whereabouts. But then I suppose I did through the agency of my platonic pal, ex of this machina, Anna. Of course, I prattled of your doings in the great green cow-pie pastures and your writing—what else to do, I had one arm, few ribs, and a radio that brought in only static and hog futures, not even a ball game. Lucy wrote to Anna or worse, Anna to Lucy. No telling the configurations of female hegemony. And she is coming to scald your hearth! Bless you, old man. I cannot claim such luck. Lovely Lucy. Lovely Anna. They have made a cad of me. No, they have made a cad of me again. Listen, the girl here who inspired me to this latest idiocy in cornfields, (what am I supposed to do here with only Mozart, who, after all, is dead) even she must be in league with those two. She has left for Boston with her biker, but not before moving out on him, moving in with me, then moving out on me (perhaps it was the Hamlet in her that first attracted me) and in this last migration, a little frenzied as you might imagine, we sense the coda, somehow, everything else having been stated in all the keys that matter, out the window, dogs are circling, spinning, toward that final steaming turd—where was I, yes, of course, I am helping her lug her things, have done all the work except for the cat, my shoulder and ribs newly, barely, serviceable—the cat breaks free in my car and, terrified by traffic, bites her, and me, her rescuer, to the bone, to the several bones. My fingers are swollen to sausages I have been shot for tetanus and for the microbes that swarm on pussy's soft pink tongue, the most hideous refuge of pestilence known to . . . oh I was revenged I pushed it out the door thinking myself mortally wounded after all blood was spurting arteries I thought the pipes had burst for sure. It was our love of drama that made us bleed so I suppose, and the cat, how she loved that cat, made the very end it must have feared, under the wheel(s) of I should like to say a quarry truck, but I don't know. In Beethoven's Fifth he gets the ending right, but in the Third you want something, more of the tonic, a bigger truck, I can't quite say. It was wheels killed the kitty and that's all the kitty needs to know. Nor did they slow much even to watch us bleed. That last E flat for me was short and a slammed door. I got my stitches and my shots and your letter. Heed (from the Old English, Irishman) me, here in this eddy off life's big circle, somewhere in the neighborhood of five o'clock, playing the Bermuda triangle, me, your friend, from days of yore (from the Middle English, or as we say around here, "belonging to you"), how can you expect your book to gush like me before a cat bite with the lovely Lucy in your bed. She'll drain you, worry your daylight hours with dusting and she'll pester you at night until the male chicken (I do not choose to name him) crows. But she is a wonderful and lovely girl. Remember me to her.

J

Ghosts

Nashville, 1985

　　I helped Karen roll up a bloody disposable hospital pad. Now that her midwife's bag was packed and all the drugstore-smelling supplies were stacked or disposed of, the room had an awkward feeling. Gwyn and the baby were resting in the living room, where the spring sunshine made warm patches on the carpeting. The bedroom, now that it was quiet, seemed cold and dark. The cradle, which I spent the last month making for the baby, rested in a corner, stacked with baby clothes like a department-store display. Karen winked at me as she headed for the door.

　　"I knew everything was going to be all right when Gwyn stood up and whizzed on the floor," she said. "Then we were in the ball game."

I watched Karen walk out the front door and wondered whether the birth of my son had been more a miracle than I had first thought. Did this woman, who lived in the country in a cabin with goats and chickens and empty guitar cases which somehow represented her absent husband, really know anything about bringing babies into the world? I had located Karen almost at the last minute, after Gwyn decided that the midwives at a nearby commune were as bad as doctors. They had insisted that Gwyn and I spend a month with them before the birth, to develop friendship, trust, the necessary bond—and Gwyn began to feel her privacy threatened. I had been disappointed—those people were like a lost tribe of the Amazon, real hippies—but my disappointment dissolved into relief. I really hadn't wanted to spend so much time away from my house and from the orchestra.

Gwyn's labor had been long and difficult, but after the episode with the amniotic fluid, the baby had come quickly. Karen swarmed over him for a moment, doing all sorts of things she had promised not to do, suctioning, probing, brandishing instruments of gleaming chrome and dull black rubber—at least it seemed so to me in my haze of exhaustion. Then it was quiet again, and a new creature looked out at the world, seeming somehow to have seen it all before.

Only a few minutes after Karen left, Gwyn was sleeping and I navigated the back patio, avoiding the puddles left from a sudden shower, holding the baby for Anna to photograph. Baby Andrew was quiet and small, and seemed relieved that his ordeal was over. He looked silky and beautiful, as fresh as the newly washed sunlight. Anna's being there was no more unusual than any of the other things that had happened since Gwyn and I had been together. Gwyn was predictably unpredictable. She had grown friendly with Anna on a trip to Philadelphia, and had invited Anna herself. Then, as if he had sensed the ideal moment, the baby had come. Anna had proven to be more useful than the midwife during Gwyn's labor. I had not been much help. My relationship with Gwyn was lousy. Of the three people in the room when baby Andrew came, I felt closest to Anna, then Karen, and finally Gwyn. Gwyn still slept soundly, her jaw grinding in determination, while I held Andrew in the late golden light behind my house.

It seemed some sort of perfect order to me to be in this place. My house was a treasure, a little rental cottage with stucco walls and a peaked roof, nearly at the top of a hill. It had been willed to me by a friend who finally decided to leave the city for Boston, suddenly filling my life with the quiet her friendship had always denied. There was a park on the very hilltop, and the backyard of the house merged with the park's greenery. There were steep stone steps from the street up to the front door, a fine stone patio in the back, and then the ascending yard which ended where the park began. According to my departed friend, there was even a ghost, an ogre in the basement, a legend which I attributed to the antique mutterings of the oil furnace. But the atmosphere could be gothic. When it rained, thunder and lightning were thickest here, because it was so high. Trees often broke in heavy winds and scattered their limbs across the winding road.

I watched Anna snapping photographs. Her dark straight hair was still clinging to her face in a few stray wisps. She had worked hardest rubbing Gwyn's back through the night and morning. Her brown eyes seemed tired but the corners of her mouth worked in a fleeting response to the tiny hands grasping their father's finger. Before we turned to go in, I spoke to her. "I love you, Anna."

She answered with scarcely any hesitation. "I love you, too."

The next day, she took a plane back to Philadelphia.

The new pediatrician rolled his eyes over the home birth, but he pronounced the baby sound and healthy. Andrew wasn't large, but he would probably grow fast. The doctor didn't have any concerns about the dimple on the baby's bottom, or his twisted leg. "It's cramped in there, young man, he'll straighten it out in time." I began to think that humans must come with a greater variety of defects than I had ever imagined.

It seemed almost inevitable, six months later, for me to find myself alone in my house, now pondering the variety of defects in my marriage, while still sharing the care of baby Andrew with

Gwyn, who had moved to the other side of town. Gwyn and I had married hastily, the baby had come unexpectedly, and the sweeping changes he brought with him seemed to have loosened the last bit of glue holding us together. My routine was to take care of the baby two days and then have two days off, rather like a fireman.

My plant room became Andrew's nursery. It had been intended as a front bedroom, but it seemed to have more windows than walls. It was in this room that I had succeeded, for the first time in my life, miraculously, in growing philodendra, African violets, ferns, and even orchids. I built wooden trays lined with plastic that I filled with flat rocks and an inch or so of water. The plants loved it. I had never cared for plants before, although Anna had always filled her house with growing things. Something about the quiet of this house had moved me to grow them, to seek them out. There were ferns hanging in front of all the windows. Andrew's crib and changing table shared space with avocado trees and standing ferns. My own bedroom was in the back, where I could lie in bed in the morning before rising and look out the back window up the hillside toward the park woods. Sometimes there would be rabbits nibbling and hopping stiffly in the grass.

Mornings I would wake and change the baby, put him in his high chair, and try him with cereal or fruit. It was odd how cycles of refusal and appetite seemed to relate to mental and physical development. Picky eating seemed to coincide with spurts of mental development: elaborate syntactical structuring of gibberish and serious sorting and emptying games with toys. A healthy appetite went with pulling up and incessant crawling. I felt I could tell what was going on in Andrew's little factory by the amount of baby food I had to scrape down the drain. After breakfast, a cleaned-up Andrew would crawl around the floor while I practiced. When there were rehearsals and concerts, I relied on the old couple across the street, the Joyces.

Mrs. Joyce had run a restaurant downtown for many years called "Sammie's Place," and she could still whip up a Southern-style meal that would leave me desiring nothing but tea and toast for a day. Mr. Joyce watched TV in a cloud of cheap pipe smoke. Sometimes he would venture out in his pickup truck, or tinker in the back shed with lawn mowers, which he repaired. He never ate with us, or paid much attention to Andrew crawling around in the living room. I tried to eat as fast as I could, keeping one eye on the baby.

I found it difficult to relax or find the rhythm of attention Mrs. Joyce seemed to have with Andrew. I had argued my competence to care for Andrew for long hours with Gwyn, but I was beginning to suspect I could compensate for my lack of natural ability only by constant and unrelenting effort. I remembered what had happened when Gwyn was packing to move out. Boxes were stacked everywhere, and, emerging from the basement, I suddenly realized I had lost track of the baby. I found him in the bedroom with a jar of boot cleaner open, and the white creamy paste smeared over his mouth and face. The people at the poison control center told me what to watch for, and I had watched and waited, but there had been no ill effects, except for my own panic. They pointed out to me that moving was a serious distraction which was often responsible for children's injuries. I felt the list of distractions might be infinite.

My days off from baby duty were often spent in sleep or in blurry puttering with plants. I found myself eating and sleeping at odd times, something which would have disturbed me deeply in former days. Once I dreamed I was packing again. At first I wasn't clear whether it was for Gwyn or for myself, but, reaching into a box, I gashed my hand on some broken glass, perhaps a mirror. I was trying to stop the bleeding when someone knocked at the door. I found myself on the road in front of my house, trying to explain to Mrs. Joyce that I was leaving. All the while the blood poured from my hand, soaking my shoes, but she didn't seem to notice. I was still trying to make her understand when I was wakened by more knocking sounds, and discovered that I had rolled over on my arm. The arm had no feeling and was useless. I had to pick it up with my other hand to move it, and then lie quietly, waiting for it to fill with the blood the dream had drained away. I thought I heard knocking again, but it was subsumed in the grinding start of the oil furnace, and I gratefully slipped back into sleep.

I often called Anna in the late evenings. She would answer in a faint, tired voice, but there was usually a bit of light in it. Enough of the old lilt to allow me to feel she was glad, or at least tolerant of my call.

"Anna, the one thing I'm afraid of is that she's going to wake up from all this fooling around and decide to sue for custody of the baby. I'll be dead in the water. This is Tennessee. She'll get the baby and my salary. She'll perch on my carcass and pull out my insides in tiny bites forever . . . Anna. Anna, are you there?"

"I'm here."

"You sound so damn faint."

"I'm very tired."

"I'm sorry. I guess you would rather not hear about all this."

"I suppose I would rather take a bath and get some sleep. Gwyn just isn't that concerned about you, I don't think. Andrew half the time is almost more than she's able to deal with now, maybe always. She needs you for him. I think your insides are safe."

"Tell that to my insides. But I'll let go. . . . Anna, will you please consider coming down here?"

There was a long silence.

"No, James. I won't come." Our late-night phone connection, faint and fuzzy, with its tiny voices in the background, seemed to fill the room. The light from the lamp around me, yellow and dusty, the noises of the house, all seemed stronger than the link between me and Anna.

"Good night, Anna."

I sat looking at the phone. The house was creaking around me as if a frost were setting in. I didn't want to go to bed, but there was nowhere else to go.

The next morning, I received a call from my landlady. She had found a buyer for the house, and she was offering me the first refusal she had once promised. Before the conversation was over I knew how long I had—less than a month—before I must move out. I wondered at her urgency. Even rich people must run out of cash, I thought.

Gwyn delivered Andrew on her way to work. It was an uncomfortable ritual with few words exchanged, like a surrender on a battleship. It was very cold outside, but I decided to take Andrew for a grocery outing and try to clear my mind. I dressed the baby and raised him to my left shoulder. The most comfortable carrying position for both of us had Andrew peering over my shoulder, with my left arm wrapped around his bottom, serving half as seat, half as restraint. This gave me a free right hand for doorknobs and car keys. The front door of the house opened inward because there was a steep, fan-shaped stone stairway down to the walk, which then wound sideways to more steep steps and the road below. As I turned to close the outside door, Andrew gave a sudden lurch, flexing his body powerfully like a fish. There was a moment when the baby was completely free in the air, then I grabbed for him with both hands. I held the baby over my head as I stumbled down the steps following the momentum of my recovery lunge. There was a terrible feeling in my nose, as if I had been punched, which came from the first unexpected jarring of my foot on the way down the steps. But I never lost my balance. At the level of the walk, I recovered myself and held the baby tightly to me with both arms. Andrew was still squirming violently. I relaxed my grip and walked back up the stairs, wondering if anyone had been watching. Inside, I put the baby down, sat in the shabby armchair, and cried. I had grabbed where I thought the baby might be, and Andrew had been there. I could see myself driving to the emergency room— with what? I thought of how simple my life would be without Andrew. Then I felt Andrew pulling at my shoelaces. I picked the baby up, and we cried together, Andrew out of annoyance.

I was sure Mrs. Joyce had seen us. I imagined her testifying in a custody hearing: "In broad daylight, in broad daylight, mind you, he was so drunk, he dropped the baby down those steep front stairs!" I decided to take Andrew down the hill and have a visit. I could chat about baby-sitting while trying to figure out whether she had seen me juggling the baby down the front steps. Mrs. Joyce was my only sitter. I had to find out if she would still be available when I moved. While Andrew chewed on the edge of the table, I learned more than I really wanted to know about baby-sitting: the availability of daughters-in-law, of more distant relatives and their pedigrees, going rates, the problems with teenagers, more trouble with teenagers. It did seem that Mrs. Joyce had not seen the near-accident. I was wondering whether I should admit I had already forgotten the names I had been given when Mrs. Joyce suddenly turned away from the sink and said, "Honey, you should get back together with Gwyn. She's a nice girl, but she doesn't know what she wants. It's all for the baby, now. You need to think about the baby."

"I don't think I could change her mind, Mrs. Joyce."

"Of course you can, honey. Mr. Joyce and I—did I ever tell you about how we got back together?"

"No."

"Well, Horace and I married young, and in a few years he got to messing around with other women, and I divorced him. Twenty years went by." There was a pause while she vigorously scrubbed at a pan in the sink. She resumed, "Horace raised his own family. I raised mine. Then my second husband passed away, and I met Horace again. He had lost his wife. We realized we still loved each other. We got married again, and we have been together fifteen years now. There is room in the human heart for many things. You can take her back. The baby needs you both."

Mrs. Joyce was so convincing, I felt a glow inside as I carried Andrew back up the steps to my house. I thought of Andrew growing up with his mother and father together. I thought of Horace and Sammie, after all that time, getting together again. I looked at the telephone and dialed Gwyn's number.

She answered, "Craig, I knew you'd call back." I held the phone for a moment before hanging up. I decided to take the baby to the grocery store, this time without incident.

That night, the baby seemed restless and would not settle down—even with music boxes and a bear with recorded human heartbeats. I jogged him up and down, pacing slowly through the house, until his crying became a rhythmic chant. The chant gradually became hypnotic and grew softer until he was finally asleep. I placed him carefully in his crib and pulled the blanket over him.

When I passed the front window, I saw it had begun to snow. I decided to call Anna in Philadelphia, but there was no answer. I built a fire with the hackberry wood I had split from a front-yard tree the wind had blown down last year. I thought about packing, but I fell asleep in the chair watching the fire. When I woke, the log had burned down to ash and the house was quiet. I felt restless. Looking out a front window I could see it was still snowing and that the steps and the walk were hidden. There was not an unpleasant feature of the landscape left, not a smudge. There were no tracks of cars, no sled tracks, no footprints. The bushes were pillows and each tree limb and twig held its own tiny mountain of snow. I could not bring myself to go out the front door, so I went to the back of the house and walked out on the patio. There was one street light near the edge of the park, but it was a distant halo, far up the hill. The snow seemed to have its own gentle glow. I began to see motion at the top of the back yard, something dark moving toward me. I stood quietly and watched. It moved steadily toward me. At first it seemed to be about the size of a cat, but it was half buried in the snow, and as it moved, it plowed a furrow. Now it was clearly larger as it worked its way down the hill, never seeing me. When it was level with me, about ten feet away, I could see it was an opossum. It made a sharp turn and plowed toward the house, then it clambered into an opening I had never noticed before in the basement wall. A snow-plowing opossum that lived in the basement. Perhaps that explained some of the odder noises in the night. So this was the ghost. I felt pleased. I began to feel the chill of a fresh wind. The lines of snow against the distant street light were bending again. I turned and went inside.

I checked on Andrew, then picked up a few stuffed toys from the floor and tossed them into the cradle in the corner of the room. I straightened the cloth that covered the frayed arms of the chair I had been sleeping in and settled myself. I heard thunder. Winter thunder. A peculiar, muffled sound, half embarrassed to be out in the world. The wind began to tangle in the casement windows and draw out thin moaning sounds. There were three distinct pitches and they vibrated as if there were an invisible harp in the room. I had once discovered I could eliminate the music by fastening the windows as tightly as possible, but it seemed wrong to deny the house its voice. This night I settled

Indonesia

Missouri, Philadelphia, Nashville, 1954–90

I did not see my friend Harold until several months after he came back from Indonesia. There was a postcard from California asking for money, but I was broke, separated from Anna, forced to spend the summer with my parents. I was in bad shape, thrown by circumstances back into the sprawling slum of my childhood. I had thought Harold was gone for good, but sometimes the river turns back upon itself.

I was tortured by my parents that summer. My father would say, "You remember Richie Weeks, who shot his leg off climbing over a fence—" And I would say, "No, no, that was Richie Berry, I never heard of Richie Weeks." And we would be off and running, arguing for hours about whether I went to school with some guy. Half the time it *was* somebody I knew once but had forgotten, my memories sealed over.

My parents, on the other hand, are all memories. They are crawling with characters from my high-school days. Why, once that same summer I decided to escape my history by declaring that I was sick and needed a week of bed rest. I *was* sick; I had made myself ill. It is an easy thing to do if you are determined enough. Anyway, after a few days, I heard a woman's voice in the kitchen, talking to my parents, really boisterous; so I staggered in to see who it was, and there was this slightly overweight woman who seemed to know me. You know, the kind who asks you something, then steps on whatever your answer might be with her next brainless outburst. After she finally left, and as I was going back into the bedroom, my mother said, in her most offended tone, "James, how could you be so rude to Kathy?" Kathy? Kathy was the red-haired girl with creamy white skin I used to undress in my car and hold in my lap like a child, naked and juicy, while we ducked from passing headlights. That was Kathy?

Kathy and I are sitting together in a one-room country church. My mind is still numbed by the peculiar sermon, which has consisted of a disparate collection of readings from magazine articles. It is this sermon, I now realize, which prefigures what I am about to say, the story I am about to tell, its very lack of structure, and especially the germ within it, the irritant, about which I will speak later: the Dalawa. And while I can remember scarcely anything of the sermon, it has left me in a certain state of mind which I will not learn to recognize until later, much later, in my life. This *is* true of our lives, that they are filled with prefigurings, most of which point to futures which never happen. The sermon has ended inexplicably, just when I thought it never would, and a hymn has begun. Perhaps "Rock of Ages" or "Bringing in the Sheaves." I begin to notice the vigorous, inaccurate style of the pianist, but I keep my eyes on my hymnal. Kathy pokes me in the ribs. I ignore her. She pokes me again. She is close enough for me to smell her breath. She smells like bubblegum. I look up just as the fat lady at the piano plays an awful discord. This is a clinker that would wake the dead, the clam of a lifetime. Kathy pokes me again. I look. The woman is staring at her music with hideous concentration, her tongue protruding nearly an inch from her fat lips. I am doomed. My shoulders begin to heave. By the time the hymn is over I cannot control my laughter. Our pew is a bit wobbly to begin with, and now it begins to shake and tremble with abandon. I bite my lip and tongue until I taste blood, but the pew keeps on shaking. Faces turn toward us.

On the way home, in the darkness of the back seat of Kathy's parents' car, she slips my hand under her dress and I fondle her as her mother continues to lecture on certain aspects of ecclesiastical propriety.

I remember when Kathy exited my life. Technically, it was my exit—I was banished. In a few weeks she learned she was not pregnant, but by then, of course, it was too late.

She had told her parents everything. It was nighttime, and I walked out of her house for the last time. There was no moon, and I looked up at the stars for a moment before I drove home. I was eighteen years old, and I remember what I felt, too. It was as big as what I saw above me, and it was all in the middle of my chest. That was when Kathy left. That chubby middle-aged woman laughing in the next room was a dream, a nightmare. I know my anger in this matter is unfair, but I am helpless before it. I cannot say whether it is directed at myself, at Kathy, or at God's pretty lights, still twinkling over the same empty fields of hay, beans, and corn that circled Kathy's house.

It is so peculiar, the ways we manage to become ourselves, the energy with which we burst overnight from the dark secret soil of the forest like mushrooms and join the world of light and birdsong, as if we had belonged there all along. I have done some such thing. We all have. But I wonder now at it. My father appeared and disappeared during my childhood in a similar sense. Not in the sense of the father who leaves his home for prison, or war, or another woman, but like some exotic fungus—something which has not been seen for years "in these parts," but which now is common, too common, underfoot. He was, I think, devoted to whatever job he had: traveling salesman (certainly good reason to be away from home), manager of a book store, positions of various responsibility in grocery stores. All of these jobs he worked at with obsessive fervor. I do not remember family outings. I do not remember him asleep on the couch. I do remember waiting with my mother for him at suppertime. Suppertime was at six o'clock. My father never appeared at six o'clock, but supper was ready, and we waited together. Later, sometimes much later, we would hear him whistling (he always whistled), and I would rush to the table, my hands washed. The meals were ordinary, with only flashes of violence. I remember dodging a pork chop once. I don't believe it had been intended for me. Another time my father slapped at my hand. I had the annoying habit of holding my bread, butter, and sugar on the back of my hand—practically everything I ate was covered with sugar. I was a picky eater, and to get me to eat, my mother sprinkled the stuff on anything it would stick to. My father intended to slap my open-faced sugar sandwich into my face, or my lap, I suppose, but I ducked and it hit the wall behind me. I do not remember what happened then.

What did my father look like? He looked like a father. I remember being fascinated that he looked as he did, and not any other way. I was fascinated that I could recognize him in a room, or on the street, not being able (as I am unable now) to picture him to myself. I believed also that my father and my mother looked alike. That all parents looked alike, as did brothers and sisters. He was powerful, but that goes without saying. His punishment was swift and unexpected, while my mother's was calculated. "Wait till I get you home. . . ." And her memory was excellent. My mother's weapons were hairbrush and comb. My father, like some symphony conductors, did not feel the need for a tool of any kind to stand between him and his art. I wholeheartedly preferred his punishment. It was over before it began.

Around the time I was in the seventh grade, my father suddenly appeared. He had been at home all along, especially since the third grade, but my main impressions had been of waiting for him at suppertime, or waiting for him in the car while he went into a store for something (he loved to talk to strangers), or those lightning moments of punishment.

He must have decided around that time that I needed his attention. He asked me if I would like to go fishing with him. And we went fishing together regularly for several years, really until I left home for college. It became another of his obsessions. In the summer we would fish every day after supper. We fished in ponds, in creeks, in rivers, in lakes. We fished at night, in the evening, early in the morning. I can see myself in a diner at four in the morning looking with horror at an enormous pile of pancakes. It was called a short stack. During the time we spent in the car, driving to various farm ponds, where my youth and innocence served as an excellent introduction to the fish-guarding farmers, my father taught me to whistle. Nothing seemed to come naturally to me, but I did manage to learn to whistle. During the time we fished together, there was silence. But we were together. He was always absorbed. I was distracted by frogs and birds, by the deep and dreadful darkness he would insist upon fishing into. I often had to beg him to go home.

"So," Harold says, "there we are finally in Indonesia, and these Germans are making a big fuss about whether we should ever eat animal flesh. They take it to Tolu. This little man, practically sitting on a throne, most of his teeth rotted out from Coca-Cola. Tolu says, 'Don't worry. It's already dead. It won't hurt you.'"

We are sitting in my kitchen in Philadelphia in our little slum house. This is during one of the times when Anna and I have decided to get back together—I'm playing the operas again—we think there will be almost enough money to live on. Anna's ferns and spider plants are drooping around us and all the air is pink from the plant lights. The walls are scraped brick. If it weren't for my toad cages, we could have been in a fancy restaurant.

Tolu is the spiritual leader of Sambilan. Harold and I began with it at about the same time, a few years before. Most of our friends as well. Sambilan was my greatest hope, and the Dalawa was its doorway. My hands trembled as I reached for the doorknob, my body trembled as it had when I first made love to Kathy, the first time I had ever made love. This was the greater entranceway. But the door opened to cold corridors and further doors. Finally I ceased to tremble and complained of headaches. Around the bend of the great river, I saw only more river. I dropped out. Harold stayed with it and eventually flew with a group to Indonesia to search out the source of the Dalawa, Tolu himself. Now he's back. I don't know what he found. I only know that some come back. Some don't.

Anna is frowning at Harold. She clammed up when he started talking about levitation. I look at Harold. Harold is nervous, but that might be the coffee. Harold consumes vast quantities of coffee. Smokes Luckies. Has curly black hair and a four-o'clock shadow. Harold's hands, fingers, are somehow still graceful despite their nervous twiddling.

"I still get the Dalawa," he says. "Sometime I'll just be standing in line at the supermarket, or giving a piano lesson, and I start to shake. My spine turns to jello."

Anna's lips tighten a little more. They're going to disappear in a minute.

Once, after a Dalawa, Harold and I sat in the big basement kitchen drinking Rolling Rock. Alcohol was forbidden by Sambilan, but we had given ourselves dispensation. We always gave ourselves dispensation. None of our other housemates were about. I had a headache. It was unpleasant for me to tilt my head back far enough to drink the beer.

"You were talking about your father," Harold said.

"What?"

"You were talking to your father. Yes, I'm sure of it."

"You're kidding. I didn't talk to anybody."

"You really don't remember?"

"I feel like shit."

Harold and I had lived the Bohemian life together as housemates for a year in a large brownstone in Philadelphia. I had supplied new poems for a half-dozen art songs he had done as settings of Rilke. There had been difficulties concerning copyrights or permission, so it was my job to put new toothpaste in the tube. The whole project fell apart when I set a particularly thunderous passage with some rather precious verbiage about butterflies. Harold was discreet in his disappointment. But our friendship was sound, and our collaborations continued all that year, some literary, some musical, all grandiose. Nevertheless, fate sprung us apart. As far apart as Indonesia and Missouri.

In the long years to come, Harold is going to take an interest in the theater. During this time he will withdraw from writing music (in the midst of working on my flute concerto), but I should be fair, this is a process, like something enormous slowing, a train grinding to a stop, sparks, steam. But this is not right. There would not be steam. Steam engines are a romance. And besides, this metaphor is all wrong, the process is slow, but there is nothing enormous and powerful about it; rather it is like a stream which is drying up, only remaining in occasional pools where tiny fish wait, not knowing why they are waiting, not knowing that they are waiting. And one day the pools are gone, and there are only stones, still damp on the bottom. The process is even as slow as this metaphor. In the details of his life, for example, Harold will break his leg at a party, dancing. I can imagine this, rather like a Dalawa, but well lit, a moment of drunken exuberance, then the awkward sprawl, the close memory of an odd sound, which was the bone breaking, and, of course, no pain. There would have been no pain at first. Then Harold will take up painting. I have a portrait on my study wall that he did of me. I look too much like Trotsky for my taste, but it holds my likeness as well, and the colors are fine. I can also imagine things for Harold which he has not done, but might.

Let us say that he and I, in a kind of sentimental attempt to recall that year we spent together, decide to present a concert of New Music in our two cities. I will be performer. Harold will be composer and accompanist. Harold will compose a new piece for this occasion. Yes, it is based on the slow movement of the Bartók Second Violin Concerto in retrograde, perhaps an odd strategy, but this is a matter of aesthetics. I am in this instance merely a performer, not a critic, and the music is difficult enough to play.

In my city we will perform in an old church, and despite the eloquent article I have written for the newspaper, less than a dozen people attend. The next day there is a sudden snowstorm and Harold's flight is canceled. We walk in the snow and watch a black dog, running full tilt, ecstatic, its nose buried in the snow, plowing a furrow. It crashes into a hedge and sprawls. We laugh. Later in the day the sun begins to warm the trees and the snow falls in large clumps, plopping to the earth. Harold suggests that there is a wonderful music in this thumping and plopping snow. I am noncommittal, fearful he will undertake to notate it.

In Philadelphia, our program is a great success, well attended, and Harold's piece earns bravos. Afterward, in a nearby restaurant, Harold becomes expansively drunk.

"Slambilan is the question for all answers," he toasts. "And the Dalmation is its begonia." Harold's friends, who have accompanied us, applaud again.

It strikes me that our performance is over, that its sounds are forever lost, and that we are reinventing it in our minds. It is becoming more and more successful. The mistakes, the omissions, the wrong entrances, the faulty intonation are all disappearing in a nostalgic haze. I try to hold on to it as it was, but like a mutating virus, it keeps shriveling, worsening—it is a terrible embarrassment, a disaster. I have either had too little or too much to drink.

Back in my kitchen in Philadelphia, Anna starts to talk to me again, and her full lips, slightly bruised, reappear, after Harold leaves . . . for what? He was still a composer then. Living alone. I would send him poems when I was on the road. Sometimes he'll come across one and send it to me. It is taking him longer to lose them than it took me.

"I'm tired of the Dalawa," Anna says. "Always it's the damned Dalawa."

"I quit. I'm done with it. I'm just waiting for it to be done with me."

"It's an excuse for male hegemony," Anna says. "All those people calling out to Allah."

"I never called on Allah. I seldom opened my mouth. You encouraged me to go. Now I have spiritual flashbacks."

(Here I am forced to dodge a wet dishcloth, which splats on the raw brick wall and clings like a living creature.)

I think the Dalawa got lodged in my lowest chakra. A sexual thing. I did not fool around much in those days. But when we made love, Anna accused me of learning things from loose women. But I *was* faithful. It was the Dalawa. I'd have gone back to ask them about it, those Sambilan people, and they'd have told me something about my body purifying itself, but it was more important (I thought) to Anna that I stay away.

Exit Anna: Anna will put up with this for a while, but there will be a scene, the two of us sitting in an azalea garden with a little fountain trickling at one end. This scene has become an icon in my work. It is harmless, like the pictures of our children we show each other in our real lives. In this scene, Anna will have told me that she is not going to follow me to the ends of the earth, not even, in fact, to the city where I have just been offered a job playing in an orchestra. We will hold hands, and cry a little more, and I will leave for that city, where I will blow the rust out of that lower chakra, and the Dalawa will subside like a flood, leaving twigs, uprooted trees, mud, dead animals, and my lovely Anna in its wake.

But not completely. Sometimes I can be sitting at my work, and a cold finger will poke me in the ribs. I'll get a letter in a few days from Harold. A poem, or a play. Harold's plays tend to the obscure—in my favorite, Quantz and C. P. E. Bach are playing poker at Sans-Souci while Frederick bulls his way through one of Quantz's three hundred flute concerti. "Rhythm? What rhythm?" C. P. E. says. "Play cards." But Harold's poems are keen, intelligent, and touch on his secret inner life, which, like any good inner life, is awash with guilt and pain. I find such things difficult. Even repulsive. I am such a prude.

I am fishing with my father at one of our favorite farm ponds. My mother has come along. She will fish only if we buy a bucket of minnows. Still fishing. She watches a red-and-white plastic bobber drift gently in the water. It is much more soothing than what my father and I do—cast artificial lures dripping with gangs of hooks, which snag moss, twigs, tree limbs, almost anything but fish. Suddenly there is a tremendous strike. My father has hooked a trophy bass. I can't believe the size of it, even from the other side of the pond where I have wandered, looking for frogs. It is jumping, standing on its tail. It won't stop jumping. I have never seen anything so awesome, so enormous.

"Get the net! Get the net! Don't just stand there, you idiot, get the net!"

Somewhere trees have been felled by this voice. I want to watch the beautiful fish dancing in rage on top of the water, but I am running up the hill to the car. At the fence I get stuck and cut a long gash in my arm on the barbed wire. When I come struggling back down the hill with the net, the fish has been beached. The fight is over. I am afraid I will not be allowed to touch it, so I do not ask. No one is interested in my scratch.

Anna says, "I thought you might find this interesting." A note clipped to a newspaper article on orchestra conductors. After years of silence. Is this Anna touching my life again? I fire off five pages pared down from twenty. To what? A box number. And silence.

Harold sends me a story about a double-bass player we both knew. The bass player calls him up, says he's blotto, he's wrecked. Needs help finding his bass. Harold goes over to help him out. It was there in the apartment. A one-room apartment. There's more to this story that I'm leaving out. There are always things left out of stories, important things, like the bass. Invisible, enormous things. We must always, however, suspect their presence.

My first Dalawa. We empty our pockets. Remove our shoes. Stand in a circle in the darkened room. I can hear the women from the next room. Many of them are already singing. I have listened to all this outside the door. To show my good faith. One month. Two months. This lovely singing coming from the one room, from high up, as if they were all moths floating about the light fixtures, clinging with flat wings to the ceiling. Now I am inside that outer door, in the room with the men. Finally. The Helper says, "Begin." I hear: moaning, snoring, snorting, belching, farting, grumbling, squeaking. From the next room—still that ethereal singing. Shadows move, some spinning like bumper cars. Eons pass. I lift one leg. I am a heron looking for frogs. I lift the other. Perhaps fish. I feel a breeze. I think for a minute, just for an instant, of lifting both my feet and rising on that wind. The next thing I know I am home, arguing with Anna. Persuading, not arguing. That she should come to the Dalawa. Anna is adamant. Suddenly I think of the Scotch telegram I used to read over the counter in the cheap restaurant where my parents would stop for coffee on the way to visit my mother's relatives. *Adamant bitter asinine places.* There was a bubblegum machine on the counter and my favorite waitress used to shake it until the best plastic toy would come out with a gumball for my penny. I could read. I read it over and over. *Anacin hospital. Adamant . . .* I must have read it a hundred times. Finally my father explained it to me.

Anna is adamant. "I will not join a religious organization which holds its meetings over a dirty-book store."

Harold and I keep cutting across each other's lives like comets. We are obviously part of some kind of gravitationally bound system. But I have not been to Indonesia or spoken to Tolu. I do not understand Harold's stories, and he does not understand my poems. I wonder if it is a kind of evolutionary trick of the human organism—this not understanding? Something that insures our survival?

Anna is silent on this. I cannot say whether she has another scene, another line. I cannot even guess if she knows this herself.

My parents are kinder now. They seldom argue with me about the identities of my school cronies. The warmest, brightest part of their light shines farther back now. Their hopes for me have been tempered by the actual. It's true that my father and I have waged a kind of unspoken battle through the years, but the fact that we do not speak of it, and continually forgive each other, is our bond.

My parents believe me when I tell them I love music. That it still makes me feel glorious. No, this is not true. They might believe me, they would like to believe me. No, perhaps they would not like to believe me. I simply can't tell what is true in this case. Sometimes the path through the forest disappears. I am, however, starting to look back on things the way they do. In fact, I pump them for history. History. I am constantly aware of the earth under me. Miles of once-living creatures compressed into the substance between me, between us, and a giant ball of glowing rock.

And what about Kathy? Kathy and my lost youth. Kathy and her lost youth, for that matter. Did I love her? Is she dusting somewhere, yelling at her kids? Do I have a right to banish her from this paragraph?

Our lives are like cats climbing trees. There is always a choice up, but no choice down, and eventually the branch diminishes and bends. Fractals. The tree shape of rivers and capillaries. And entropy. One way up, no way down, everything scattering, losing energy. Actually, and I am not alone in believing this, there may always be some order to be found, the possibility of order, in a fairly small assortment of events. However, in this instance, perhaps the narrative principle might be better served by my reintroducing Kathy to my life. I must make my argument then. Another scene.

Anna and Kathy around the little table in the pink light. The toad cages are terrariums filled with philodendra and, of course, those warty and nocturnal little burrowers chosen not for their physiognomy, but for their fine singing voices. Some croak like dinosaurs, others trill. They could fool canaries. I know of one that did. There is nothing in all of creation that says "Rivit."

Anna is solicitous of me in this scene. As I gesture and rant about the compressed miles of limestone under our feet. "Our ancestors, our families!" I insist. Anna pats my hand. There are tears in her eyes. She sees no one else at the table.

Kathy is going on nonstop. "Did you know I was dating your friend Tom?" she says in a whiny voice. "On Saturday nights when your parents wouldn't let you have the car? Besides, my mother didn't want me to go out with you. All your father's people are married cousins."

"And you lived downwind from the biggest pig farm in the county."

"What are you babbling about?" Anna looks terribly worried. "Please don't go back to Sambilan. Promise me you won't do the Dalawa anymore."

"I won't, I won't. Too many years have gone by. There is no one sitting at this table with me. No one is here, not even you. It was a fantasy. I was dreaming."

So many car trips. We were rural commuters. My mother's people lived in one small town and my father's in another. And all the fishing spots in between. I would stare out the window into the passing clumps of woods, wondering what I would find if I could wander there. Snakes and salamanders under logs. A fox or a bobcat. Another field. In winter the black trees and patches of snow. The desolation of those naked tree shapes. Sometimes, oddly, just one, alone in the center of a great empty field. The sound of the wheels on the pavement not hiding those transverse bumps of tar that stripe the road.

Harold writes again. No psychic warning this time. "Don't die on me," he says. "Everyone whose work I read I discover is a dead poet." The letter is so disturbing I dream of my father's death. I become over-cautious, drive under the speed limit. My life is unfinished. My speculations about its old players, Kathy and Anna, are mere nattering. Something else is more important.

I'm cleaning out my desk. In the back of a deep drawer there is a volume of Ezra Pound inscribed "To my one true love." Kathy? But no, there is a picture of another girl in a swimsuit between the pages. Did she give me the book? Was I her one true love? Do I have an obligation to avoid her life, to protect her feelings, or will I some day blunder into its orbit, ruining things like a skunk-sprayed dog? Perhaps in writing this I have done exactly that. It is an old book now, the pages tend to break.

Once Kathy wrote me a poem in which the phrase "limpid dishrag" occurred.

"Limpid means clear," I said.

"You spoil everything," she replied.

Harold writes again. He's on the train. Like me he was cleaning his desk and found my poem about my poetry group. This guy in the group is reading a poem which begins, no kidding, "O bury me with Shelley in the wind striped sand." It's a true story, mind you, but Harold is reading about it in my poem. I told the guy to try "O baby, bury me with Shelley in the wind striped sand." Harold says in his letter that he heard horrible laughter. Then he realizes that he is laughing. Then gibberish. It's the Dalawa. Some folks leave the car. A crazy old bag woman walks down the aisle. She gives him a look that signifies she understands everything. Sounds like a dream, doesn't it. But Harold doesn't lie.

It's the first gloom of evening, a little after supper, and I'm sitting on my own front porch with my parents. They have visited for the birthday of a grandchild. It is late enough for insects to be singing in the trees and a small opossum to be cautiously eating cat food from a dish on the other side of the porch. My father and I have shouted at each other during the evening meal. This time it is he who is feeling most guilty, but we are both probing for a way to make up. My mother can't decide what she wants to happen, but this man has lived with her almost fifty years. She will defend him like a tiger if it's not her own aggravation at stake. In the end, we don't say much, he and I.

Tolu, Tolu. What must I learn in this life? Why can't I remember the words of its sermons? Why has the Dalawa deserted me? I see volcanoes shrouded in mist. Jungles. Giant butterflies settling on the feces of some loose-limbed predator. What do I know of Indonesia? Perhaps, at the very least, the Coca-Cola comes in the heavy glass bottles I remember from my childhood.

I remember a dream, the night we sat on the porch, the night of that argument, the opossum eating the cat's food. I think it was that night. The opossums come and go, season after season, always attracted by cat food. Some have been huge. This one was small. I am sure that this is what helps me to remember. They are bold, they come early in the evening, almost glowing in darkness, ancient, ancient, small-brained creatures. Crepuscular. The heavy crepe of night lowering, its creaking masked by a conspiracy of tree crickets and cicadas.

In the dream my father was singing a song, teaching it to me, perhaps. And it was amazing, complex—somehow a thing I had almost heard in the Dalawa. I was moved to tears by this dream. It actually happened. It has forced itself into this narrative. Sewing the scenes together, I prick my finger. The little point of pain, the tears, real. Life reminds, reminds. But I think—did I truly hear a song? What were the words? The melody? I do not remember. Did I wake and forget the actual event, or did I wake (remember that I said this actually happened) from a fiction? The dream which actually happened contained nothing. No song. No words. Just the deep conviction, the profound fiction, that it had all happened.

I think that, once more, I will return to that porch and sit quietly with my parents in the darkness, the life of the night gathering around us. We will say nothing, perhaps think nothing. We will wait for a while, not a long time, but long enough to get a little sleepy, until the moment when someone breaks the silence, rises, and moves toward the warm yellow light inside the house, where time is passing—

Raag Yaman

Missouri, 1993

I have pulled the car over to the side of the road so I can watch the birds. There is a flock of what I imagine must be blackbirds or starlings, and they seem to be immensely high. I have stopped because I have never seen such a large flock of birds before. There must be tens of thousands of them. And because the flock is so high, or because the winds up there are so strong, the shape of the flock keeps changing. I can't describe what it is like—a ribbon, smoke, no, something more animated than smoke, something violently altering its shape, an amoeba on speed. But it's a serious thing, nothing to joke about. Perhaps it's an illusion, but I can sometimes see one larger bird leading the flock, being pursued, enveloped, by the flock—I think I have read somewhere that smaller birds will sometimes chase crows—or was it owls? The birds are so high they disappear when they form a certain angle with the sun. This is why I have stopped my car. Thousands of birds disappearing in an instant in the air above me. I stop and watch until they appear again, as I know they must. They are plunging through the air high above me, in agony or in joy, I have no way of knowing. Passing trucks rock my small car, which I have parked on the shoulder as far from the highway as I can manage. The birds disappear and reappear several times. The situation seems intensely dramatic, but I realize I am not going to see its resolution. I am procrastinating. I start my car and re-enter the traffic, the birds still flaring and disappearing above me. What must they see? What are they doing?

My father had called me the day before and told me I'd better come. My mother had been asking for me, and we both suspected, hoped, that my presence would cheer her. The cancer had disappeared, but she was still losing weight. I was driving to Missouri, a day's journey, with a change of clothes hurriedly stuffed into a bag and a shoebox of tapes to listen to in the car. This was a trip I had taken countless times since I moved to Nashville. In the old days the drive was longer, but more interesting—winding two-lane roads, a ferry across the Ohio, the rich cornfields and bottom lands of southern Illinois and Missouri. I've made the trip on a three-cylinder Yamaha motorcycle without a windshield, assailed by the fly-off gravel of quarry trucks and the occasional unfortunate bee. I've made it stoned, singing along with Bob Dylan in my old blue Pacer, the Studebaker of the '70s.

This time the trip was all interstate, first through the broad roadcuts in the hills west of the Cumberland River, then winding so efficiently around large artificial lakes as to render them invisible, skirting small cities, moving north, through southern Illinois (where I stopped for the birds), then west, across the Kansas-like plains of central Illinois, through St. Louis, then farther west, the traffic gradually thinning until the land becomes almost as flat as Illinois again. Except for St. Louis and the last hour of driving in Missouri, during which time I am usually confused by habit and nostalgia into that momentary pleasure I once experienced when I was a homesick college student returning— the trip was dull, monotonous—hours of endless pavement without even much traffic, relieved only occasionally by twisted black shapes of thrown truck retread, looking more animated than the usually unrecognizable road kills. Crows rose and settled professionally as I passed. My coffee tasted of the plastic thermos cup. I didn't want to think about where I was going.

After I pulled back on the pavement, after the vision of the birds, I reached into the shoebox and stuffed a tape blindly into the cassette player. I had taken the wrong box. Instead of jazz tapes, this was an archive box—I was listening to a recording of the raga Shri played by the great Indian flutist Pannalal Ghosh. I sighed, and then, resigned, listened to it, and afterward to the raga Yaman, or Raag Yaman, as I remember is written on the record. This is the sort of music I do not hear often in the world these days, not in my house, where I have carefully filed away the two or three recordings of Pannalal Ghosh that are available (I once received a letter from India, from the Pannalal Ghosh Society, seeking information on recordings of his playing), nor even in those cheap Indian restaurants which appear and disappear in cities like mushrooms in the lawn over the buried ghost of a tree stump. I played the music loud enough for it to rise above the sound level in the car, but the sound of the drone, the tambura, is really not far divorced from road noise—wind, tires rushing, fleeing but always present. The sound of that large low-pitched bamboo flute was still hypnotic, syllables rather than pitches changing, wolf mouthings, moving into and away from the province of the drone in the discrete pictographs of the raga, but every pitch rounded and shaped, as if by the working of wind and water, of time itself. It had been a long time. Then the tabla entered as the music progressed, and its tinny sound reminded me that I was listening to a recording of a recording over the shrill highway noise of a compact car. The music faded, as if my waiter had arrived and I had been served my entrée of ancient curried rooster, the flesh falling from the bone in flickering candlelight, the chutney not Major Grey's, but some vile lemon pickle tasting of kerosene.

I began to think of Anna and Sanjiv and the younger sister, Kalika. I was looking at the bare trees along the roadside, thinking of that journey from root to leaf, how paths are chosen or not chosen. Yet the tree will be a tree with its aura of leaves, tree shape, leaf shape. Something clearly recognizable has been defined, not defined by the choices of the journeys, but by the journeys themselves. It was not what happened briefly one afternoon between me and Kalika that shaped my life with Anna. But it was, I suppose, part of the shape, part of the music that now was ending and threatening to play again, until I reached out of my reverie and turned off the radio. Sanjiv was gone, he and his family, from my life. I have not heard a word from him since that summer. But Anna writes occasionally. She seems to guard her life from me—only a box number, no telephone. Her letters say nothing—I think I am more curious now that my life has slowed a little. I want to know things—what is she doing? Who is she with? Why does she bother to send these cheery, empty little notes?

The bamboo flutes I made to play that music are gone, too. The last of them cracked a dozen years ago, when I was on tour and the heat went off in my apartment. It was a handsome piece of work, a yard long, thinned from the inside to sound nearly as loud as the flutes Pannalal Ghosh played. It was the low pitch, the great length of those flutes which seemed to me to give them their magic. I tried for years to make one which would play the music I heard on that recording Sanjiv first played for me. Knowing nothing of Indian music, I laboriously notated it, intent on performing it as if it were a Western composition. The flutes I made could not be played, my hands were several inches too small. I did not have the patience to stretch my fingers as I had been told the Indian flutists did. (And I was afraid, remembering the story of Robert Schuman.) Finally I settled on moving two of the holes to the underside of the flute so I could use my thumbs as well as my fingers. I was limited in rapid passages, because I could no longer hold the flute so easily, but I could attempt to play the alap (the slow beginning) of each of the two ragas. I never performed the music, but I played it often for myself, pretending that it opened vistas of understanding for me, into the nature of music, the nature of all things. Perhaps it did. My hands ached afterward as if I had done some real work. Eventually, I moved from the life of a partially engaged freelance player to the busier schedule of a symphony musician. I no longer had time for my bamboo flutes. When I returned from that tour and surveyed the water damage in my apartment, I found that flute still hanging on the wall, cracked from top to bottom and opened up as if it were a scroll and its inside held some secret message for me to read. There were odd little lines inscribed on the surface of the flute's once-hidden insides. I couldn't decide whether I had caused them making the flute or whether they had been there all along. Surely this is my fortune, I thought, staring at the inscrutable symbols before I dropped the broken bamboo into the trash can.

I stopped once for gas, discovering how cramped my body had become, and how much colder it had grown—I had driven into another weather system, and for the rest of the trip my car was buffeted by swirling winds. After St. Louis, the traffic was unusually heavy, and I welcomed the distraction.

My father had given me directions to the county hospital, a new building in a new location, but I ignored them and took the same back road I have always taken as a short cut from the interstate, and then I drove through the length of the town. I have always loved driving down Elm Street with its deep lawns and handsomely restored Victorian houses. Closer to downtown, I drove past our big white house, hoping I'd see my father's car, but the driveway was empty.

The hospital was a mile outside of town, a warren of one-story buildings set far back from the road, an unsatisfactory cross between a motel and a country club. As I pulled into the landscaped entryway, I saw my father driving toward me. We pulled up alongside each other like two ships at sea. My father rolled down his window.

"You're too late, she's gone."

"What?"

"She had to have emergency surgery. We waited as long as we could. She's in recovery now. She doesn't have a chance."

"You said she was gone."

"She doesn't have a chance to recover from major surgery—they had to take out part of her intestines. She's got no immune system left . . ."

He began coughing and banged his hand on the side of the car in frustration. "Come on back to the house with me, I'm going to change clothes. We can't see her, anyway."

The house was dark and dusty. I realized I had never been in this house when it was dirty. My mother was a compulsive house cleaner.

She liked to iron—isn't that an odd thing, someone liking to push an iron around. I could tell it, somehow—her mood would change when she had finished the chores she didn't especially like—she would set up the long ironing table in a bright place, it made a creaking, ratcheting sound as the legs unfolded. Then she'd iron while I played my records and did homework—we listened to everything—Beethoven symphonies, Brahms, Rachmaninoff, even Berg and Webern. She never complained; the records had been her gift, a record-of-the-month club. And I would play for her. Her favorite was Mozart, the flute concerto in D. The iron making that hissing steam noise when she set it on end—the only thing windier than my flute.

I was wandering around, looking at the photographs of my parents as children, handsome antique productions standing on handsome antiques, little tables of swirling walnut and marble, when the phone rang. My father was in the shower, so I answered. It was my uncle, my mother's brother, from the hospital. We should come back to the hospital as soon as we could. The doctor wanted to talk to us.

The doctor said she had gone through the operation remarkably well. He had removed a section of her large intestine—her signs were good, he felt that he had been wrong to be so pessimistic before—she had an excellent chance for recovery. The relatives, two brothers, their wives, and a cousin, bundled themselves up and disappeared like leaves before a gust of wind. She was going to be all right. They were tired—this had been grim business, and now it was put off indefinitely—they did not want to see her in the intensive care unit, she would be asleep anyway. My father and I peered into the darkened room. One of the nurses beckoned. It was a large room, but there was only one bed, a bank of monitors behind it, glowing numbers and graphs, flashing lights. She was hooked up to a respirator, a ventilator, the nurses called it. A plastic tube was taped in her mouth and a flexible hose extended to a small square machine which made awkward mechanical noises in the midst of all that electronic beeping and light display. Her thin chest rose and fell as the ventilator did its work. She might have been playing a bassoon. Her eyes were partly open, but it was clear she was unconscious. Her hair had begun to grow back from the chemotherapy; there was half an inch of wispy down. We stood for a few minutes, my father and I, saying, each of us, something encouraging to her—the sort of thing you say in front of strangers to a person you love who is unconscious, who is probably unconscious. One of the nurses, who said his name was Joe, said we could come in any time since there was no other patient in the ICU. He said we could, *should* go home and sleep because she would be under heavy sedation, that he would call us if anything changed. She seemed very small, weighing only a little over eighty pounds, my father told me. The heaving of her chest as the ventilator filled it seemed incongruous. Her hand was warm and a glowing light extended from her forefinger, like ET, something which indicated the function of the monitors, I supposed. My father and I walked together to the parking lot and I noticed that he was limping. He said that he had fallen a few days before, crossing the street at the corner by our house. He couldn't stop marveling at my mother's amazing recovery.

"She wanted to wait for you to come, but there wasn't time. We talked about it. The surgery was her only chance and she took it. 'Let's go for it,' she said. She's tougher than she looks, that woman."

"You should know," I said, and I hugged him. It took him a long time to ease himself into the car.

At home, we heated soup, which neither of us could finish, and went to bed early. My father said he hadn't slept the night before. He was obviously exhausted.

Too keyed up to sleep, I began to wander around the house. It was an old house which once had a large yard like the ones on Elm Street, but its proximity over the years to the downtown business block, and particularly to the movie theater, caused it to lose its grandeur. Now it abutted a parking lot and a furniture store where the bulk of the lawn used to be. It still had a large front door with etched glass and a few stained-glass windows, but it had been improved rather than restored through the years. And the improvements, notions of their own times, had proven to be less than a match for the extremes of Missouri summers and winters. I wandered through the big, high-ceilinged rooms and admired walnut beds with fancy woods in the headboards, blanket chests and sideboards, and dozens of those little tables, posed like dancers, each displaying a few glass treasures, beginning, probably for the first time, to collect the dust that drifted down from the old furred rafters. I remembered clearing pigeons out of the attic space above the second floor only a few years before. I had had no idea how large the house was up there, and the bubbling sound of the pigeons, the snapping of their wings as they fled, filled me with apprehension. We had rented out the upper story when I was a child—sometimes it was simply empty. My parents never used it for living space until I went away to college.

I found an ancient bottle of Jack Daniels and poured myself a drink. Then I went down to the basement. The basement had a dirt floor with a main room where my father kept his workbench and tools, the place where he repaired old furniture. There were other rooms branching off, rooms branching from rooms, almost like catacombs. Still, it wasn't as creepy as the attic. In the room nearest the workbench, my father had stacked his wood, old and new projects. There were even some things I had left for storage in a far corner. There was a sheet of lead Anna had intended for some sculpture project—I could not remember what. Perhaps I should return it to her, or at least write her and ask her if she wanted it. And there was a tall basket with several pieces of bamboo resting in it. I set down my drink on the workbench and brushed the spiderwebs out of the way. Two of the tubes were large and not cracked, each at least a yard long. These had come from decorator-supply stores in Philadelphia. They were part of the cache of cane I had put together when I was trying to make Indian flutes. Then I heard my father calling me from the top of the stairs. He had heard me prowling around—with his teeth out, his voice seemed petulant—was I all right? I brushed my hands on my pants and went up to bed.

The next morning Joe told us she had had a good night, that he was gradually reducing oxygen from the ventilator so he could take her off aided breathing later that morning. She was awake and seemed alert. Of course she couldn't talk, there was a plastic tube down her throat, but she could nod her head a little and wrinkle her eyebrows. Several times Joe reminded her not to try to talk—I couldn't hear a sound or notice what the clue was to him. Perhaps he was just reminding her. I wondered if it hurt to try to speak. She did not seem to be able to squeeze my hand, but her hand was warm. I remembered how thin her hands had seemed to me when I was a child. They were always moving nervously, grasping things, her cigarettes, her hairbrush, playing cards in Saturday-night bridge games—I remembered hearing the crisp sound of the cards shuffling from the next room where I was gradually falling asleep, comforted by the dim babble of distant adult voices—only the sound of the cards seemed close, stacked and separated, manipulated by clever fingers. Now those fingers lay in my hand, warm and slightly swollen. She could not seem to move them. But she could lift her arm a little. Perhaps it was all she cared to try. We talked to her as best we could, but after a while she seemed dreamy and unresponsive, so we went to the cafeteria for breakfast. A year before, when my parents called me about the diagnosis and we were all three talking on the phone (a dangerous arrangement, because my mother and father would usually start to argue), was the only time I can remember her crying. She was afraid of the chemotherapy, of nausea, of getting sick. She just broke down—I told her I was sure it wasn't so bad, wondering if I could get her some marijuana. As it turned out, she didn't have that problem, not until the end, anyway.

I had only coffee, but my father had a big breakfast with some kind of gravy poured over biscuits; and we sat with the Methodist minister, a hungry and hearty man, whose bulging mouthfuls of ham and eggs did not deter even slightly his constant flow of bad jokes. He said my mother was a favorite of his, that he would check in with her later.

When we returned to the ICU there was a great deal of activity. My mother had been disconnected from the ventilator, but she still had a plastic tube protruding from her mouth. Joe explained that this was a trial run, she could be hooked back up if she could not adjust to breathing on her own. A doctor, the surgeon who had spoken with us the day before, came in and left. He seemed content to leave the decision making to Joe and two other nurses, who bustled about, notating readouts. After a while, the doctor returned and asked us to wait outside. In another twenty minutes he joined us in the waiting room and we sat on the bright blue-and-red cushions of the sturdy maple institutional furniture next to the empty nurses' station. He spoke slowly and loudly, as if he were in another room. He told us they had reconnected my mother to the ventilator. She was having problems with fluid in her lungs, which the pressure of the ventilator had been keeping in check, okay? She wasn't ready to breathe on her own yet. He said that fluid like this was a natural part of the post-operative process, and that it might be several days before it subsided. He would try again to get her off the ventilator as soon as she was able, okay?

We spent the afternoon with her, holding her hand, talking to her. At times she seemed tired of having to deal with us, but at least she wasn't uncomfortable. She shook her head no when we asked her if she was in pain. Joe was on a twelve-hour shift, and we stayed that day until the night nurse came on. We talked with him, while he straightened her IV and checked the monitors. He promised to call us during the night if there were any problems, and we went home exhausted again.

Now, it seemed, recovery was going to be several days away. She had endured a full course of chemotherapy and then radiation for the two tumors in her lungs. One, a small cell carcinoma, the nasty one, disappeared early in the treatment. The other, a slow-growing tumor, was treated with radiation. They had to move her pacemaker from one side to the other for the radiation treatment, a final indignity. After all this, she had complained of stomach pains and nausea. The oncologists seemed less interested in seeing her since her cancer was in remission, and it was only at the last moment that the abdominal infection was detected.

My father raged about the incompetence of doctors. He had taken care of her through all the treatment, but the strain showed. When he bent to kiss her, she would turn her head away—he was too solicitous, his kindness seemed guilty. She had been quieter in the last few years, reading and gardening. I enjoyed her company, especially if she wasn't complaining about my father. What parent could resist complaining to an only child? They probably did not see it as complaining, anyway. My father had ruled by temper. He did not hit, but his anger came without warning—he yelled, he bullied. We had been trained to fear it, its suddenness. In later years he had mellowed, moderated his habits, but it was still impossible to talk to him. He and I had had two or three serious conflicts since I left home, and in each one I could not bring him to acknowledge his behavior, the behavior I had finally begun to challenge; each time I had to back down. There was simply too much to lose. It was also clear to me that my mother would never take any advice I gave her when she complained to me. Finally, we had all reached this compromise. We complained as little as possible, we forgave as soon. But everyday life is not perfect. Now, even with the tube in her mouth, I could see the old tensions still playing out.

This night my father and I ate in his favorite restaurant at the local truck stop.

"Did I tell you about my fall?" he asked—then, without giving me time to reply, "I was crossing the street in the block south of the house with all those uneven cobblestones. I wanted to say something to Lloyd Smith. He was driving by in his pickup. The one with only half a bumper. What an eyesore. You remember Lloyd Smith? His kids went to school with you. You remember Hazel Smith, don't you?" I shook my head. "Well, she was in your class. I'm sure of it." A temper was creeping into his voice, like the water stains on the wallpaper at home. "What did you do when you were in school, anyway? Are you the same kid that used to live in this house?"

He was interrupted by a woman patting him on his shoulder and asking him about my mother. This was the beginning of a parade of concerned friends and neighbors. My father's description of what had happened began to lengthen with practice and become less factual.

"Oh, she was near death. She had . . . what do you call it?"—prodding me; I feigned ignorance—"Well, they had to take out a section of her intestine a yard long. It had burned through. It was terrible." Through all this the listener kept patting him and cooing softly.

At first I tried to interrupt—I wanted to say that my mother was holding her own, it seemed important to me, but after a while I realized that wasn't the issue. It was something else. Something creepy and confidential. Or perhaps sympathy. Sympathy and imagination. By the time we left the restaurant, I was exhausted again.

That night I warned my father I might be puttering around in the basement, but he seemed too tired to care. After he went to bed, I made myself another drink and went directly to the basement. One of the bamboo tubes still had the ink marks I had made to approximate the position of the finger holes. I plugged in an electric drill, found a small dull bit, and drilled the starter holes. I had discovered long ago that a sharp bit would cut too fast, that it would almost certainly catch in the strong fibers and tear or crack the cane. I think the Indian flutemakers burned the holes in their flutes. There was a time when I wanted to go to India and learn such things, to find the cane myself, the wonderful, light, straight-grained cane of Pannalal Ghosh's flutes, but Anna was against the idea. Something in me was opposed to the notion as well—it was music I was after. The adventure of the music ended when I put the flute down—India would not be put down—it had not completely escaped me that Sanjiv had dedicated his life to bringing his family out of India.

I found a metal rod and used it to break the inner partitions at the joints of the cane. There was a papery, pulpy substance blocking the hollow core of the cane at the joints, relatively easy to remove. The cane thickens at the joint segments on the outside and on the inside, and this was the flaw in my bamboo. I needed for the bore of the flute to be smooth and uniform—these swellings would muffle the tone and play havoc with the uniform placement of the tone holes. I could only hope I had chosen a piece of bamboo that would work as a flute—there was no way to know that until all the work was completed. Since one of the ends of the tube had already been opened, my first task was to remove the cottony spider nests that had colonized it. First they stuck to the tool, then to the cane, then to the tool again. I didn't want to touch them. I wondered if there were eggs or baby spiders inside. Finally I scraped them onto the bottom of my shoe and ground them into the dirt floor.

I had been listening to the tape in my car on trips to the hospital. My father and I were using our separate vehicles so we could spell each other for naps—now we seemed to be eating and sleeping inordinately. From so much listening, I suppose, I had retrieved in my mind the picture of Pannalal Ghosh from the record jacket. There is a band of yellow at the top of the jacket with *Pannalal Ghosh* in large black script written over it. The bulk of the jacket is a portrait of the great man, holding an enormous bamboo flute—not jointed, fishing-pole bamboo like mine, but perfectly straight fibers from top to bottom—probably chosen from hundreds of blanks, the rarest of the rare. I am sure the master made his own flutes. His face seems calm, the eyes dark, without focus, almost like my mother, whose eyes never quite closed as she moved in and out of consciousness. His nose is broad and his face is smooth and wide. His lips form a beatific smile—although he has raised the flute to his lips, he has not yet pursed them into the slight distortion necessary to direct air into the flute. His right hand is blurred and cut out of the picture, but his left hand, the hand closest to his face, seems small, the index finger tapering abruptly. There is an elegant ring with a stone on that finger. And his left hand, oddly, points back toward his face, a position which Western flutists do not assume—it would seem to make for awkwardness at the wrist—I was never able to resolve the mystery of it. On the back of the jacket there is some confusing explication of the raga system. I remember only a section titled "Artiste," in which some reference is made to his recent untimely death in New Delhi. I do not need to play the tape of this music any longer to hear it. Anna and I would play it for friends. We would smoke marijuana and listen to it, make love listening to it. I remember buying a second record when the first became unplayable.

The next morning we overslept, and when we knocked softly at the door of the ICU there was no response. We let ourselves in and found Joe almost wringing his hands.

"She had a rough night," he said, "and her temp's gone haywire."

"What is it?" I asked.

"One-oh-four and change," he said as he bustled about. To another nurse: "Get me some ice packs and a floor fan."

She seemed the same to me, her chest filling up like a frog's throat, almost vibrating with relief when the pressure was released—but she didn't respond when I called into her ear. Joe packed ice bags around her, under her arms and against her chest. I noticed that the outline of her pacemaker stood out on her chest like a pack of cigarettes. Her hands seemed more swollen then they had the day before. Joe set up a floor fan, and immediately tripped over the cord as he rushed to turn off an alarm. Alarms, various beeps and buzzes, kept going off. It seemed more a testing or even a malfunction of the mechanism than something useful, not really a warning. In an hour her temperature had gone down to 101 and was still falling. Joe said the lab report indicated that this was a variety of E. coli which was especially nasty, that this was the last antibiotic, a particularly expensive one, which had a decent chance of working.

"Look!" Joe said, jubilantly. She was moving her head, she was awake. We told her that she had had a bad spell, but that things were okay now, that she needed to rest and get her strength so she could get off the respirator. She nodded and drifted off. Joe had mentioned "the congestive heart failure" as one of the problems he was dealing with as he stumbled over the fan cord carrying ice packs. It occurred to me that it was a term he might have avoided using if he were not so distracted. At least I would have appreciated one of his careful explanations.

In the afternoon, instead of going home for a nap or shower, I walked around outside the hospital. There was a fitness trail for walkers, soft cedar chips underfoot. Little brushy trees lined the trail, and meadows of knee-high grass and scratchy weeds quivered under a freshening wind. I came upon a contraption like a swing set, constructed of stained or treated beams. I read the confusing instructions and decided I was supposed to hang from it, something I would have done naturally when I was a child. I could feel the joints in my shoulders and my back stretching. I popped like the old white house, which was always settling.

Still, I felt a fool—I could see myself hanging from one side, then the other, like a bored kid alone on the playground. I forced myself to keep hanging on, my feet dragging in the cedar chips— little by little, my joints loosened, I felt as if my very bones were lengthening. When I was a kid, I would have let go and run—I could see myself running gracefully across the meadow, sometimes leaping over bushes like a dog after a rabbit—but it was awkward to let go. I stumbled. My knees cracked again. I brushed my clothes as if I had fallen. A meadowlark shortened its song. I tried to find it in the field, but I could see nothing but swaying grass and weeds. The air smelled like cold mud. There was a leaden front gathering in the west.

Later that afternoon, she had several responsive moments— my father spent more time talking to her than he had before. He had overcome the awkwardness of it all, and except for forgetting that he was holding his hat, and wringing it over and over in his fingers, which made him seem as if he were begging, he did well. His voice remained cheerful. She only turned away from him once.

I decided that I would read to her the next day. There was a new night nurse, so we stayed a while and talked. Like the others, she promised to call us. I was certain that no one would call, whatever happened. We ate in the restaurant again, and fewer people accosted us this time—my father didn't have an opportunity to work up to his epic. His eating had become remarkably slow. I remembered that my mother had complained to me about it.

He turned to me with an urgent look on his face, then continued to chew—it took a long time. I waited.

"Did I tell you about my fall?" he said. "Those cobblestones on lower Elm Street are really bad. I was walking across the street to talk to somebody, that guy who fixes TV sets, I can't think of his name right now. . . ." He shoveled in another forkful and chewed until he was finished. "And I stepped where there should have been road but there wasn't, there's a dip where the cobblestones have settled, and the next thing I knew I was lying in the road. My knee is black as a bad persimmon."

"Has anybody looked at it?" I asked.

"Yeah, Doc Jenkins says I've got a cracked kneecap, and that I ought to stay off it, but how am I going to do that? Maybe I'll sue the city." He speared his mashed potatoes and resumed chewing.

That night I went out and got another bottle of Jack Daniels. Then I settled in the basement, peaceful among the raw beams and the bowed dirt floor. I nearly finished carving the blow hole with my pocketknife. We call it the embouchure hole—when I was a child learning to play the flute, I thought it was called the armature. Odd, rather than serving as armor, it is an absence, it accepts the moving air which flutters like a moth at the window, and if the work has been done properly, creates a standing wave, the sound of the flute.

The next day, Dr. Bannerjee, the surgeon (only now do I notice the irony, the man was Indian), took us aside and discussed my mother's prospects. He said he was still hopeful he could get her off the respirator. The edema was subsiding and Joe had reduced her oxygen intake to seventy percent. He seemed to be accustomed to explaining things in very simple terms. He said he was going to try the next day, okay? I realized that everything he said ended in "okay?" A kind of rhetorical punctuation, too loud, with a rising inflection. He had no idea what an annoying habit it was.

I had gone to the library and checked out *Great Expectations*. I was going to read to my mother. It was mid-morning, and the rain was coming down in thick sheets. There was a leak by the front door of the hospital, and water stood on the floor. There was no receptionist in sight. A mop and bucket stood there also, abandoned.

"Would you like me to read?" I asked her. She nodded. I was halfway into the first page before I remembered that Pip is in the cemetery, contemplating the gravestones of his parents. "Late of this parish." What could I have been thinking? I began leaving out sentences, skipping over paragraphs. Pip is hanging upside down—over what? A ventilator? What a disaster. I asked her if she was tired. She nodded. I couldn't help seeing the way she frowned as I began reading the churchyard scene. What was his name . . . Magwitch. "I wish I was a frog or a eel," he said as he stumbled off into the nettles. I looked out the dark window into the rain and wished for myself the same.

That night I found a wonderful old round file that could be used to remove the vestiges of partitions inside the tube of cane, and perhaps slightly reduce the swelling of the hard cane itself. I must be cautious because too much pressure from the inside will crack the flute—even a small crack will render it useless. Then I began carefully to enlarge the fingerholes—the larger the hole, the higher the pitch of the note which comes from it. Unfortunately, the hole cannot be made smaller. Something about files— when I was in shop in the eighth grade we had to learn about the kinds of files, the most memorable of which was "bastard file." We thought that was wonderful. I remember the titters and knowing glances. I don't remember now what characterized the varieties, perhaps this was a bastard file. I made a breadboard. It earned a C plus, which disappointed me, but I gave it to my mother anyway.

The next morning the readout on the ventilator said 100 percent. It had come to be the first thing I looked at when I came into the darkened room. I was beginning to feel I understood the science of our waiting. Joe said that she had had an odd night. He didn't think she slept much, he said, as he worried with her covers and her IV connections. He just couldn't tell, he said, it was an odd thing. He also seemed concerned about her blood pressure and discussed a different medication with Dr. Bannerjee. This, from the doctor's reaction, I surmised, was a breach of etiquette. There was no more talk of removing the ventilator. I noticed that the insides of my mother's lips seemed bruised and bloody from contact with the plastic tube. Joe said that in a long-term situation a tracheotomy would have to be performed. While we were talking, the flexible plastic hose fell off the tube in her mouth. I put it back on. It was clear plastic, probably disposable, like a cheap child's toy. The doctor looked up from the desk at the other side of the room where he had been working on a log and said, "There's an alarm for that. You needn't worry." Outside it was still raining.

There were as many as four days of rain, I can't say exactly. During that time my mother made one last gradual recovery—it seemed for a day or so that we might be able to try taking her off the respirator again, but then she began to fail again as gradually. Her blood pressure, her urine production, all her bodily functions seemed to be under the control of the doctor and the nurses.

It was as if they were playing her like a fish. But if she were a fish, she was at a great depth, and could not be brought to the boat, or even within sight. We talked to her, we held her warm hand, and her dark eyes, half hooded by the lids, seemed no longer to see anything. Evenings, after my father had gone to bed, I wandered through the empty house, always, finally, settling into the basement to carve at my bamboo flute. I found a wine cork to plug the top end, and I played it quietly, only making enough sound to tune the scale for the raga Yaman, the notes of the natural minor scale—on the piano, the white notes from A to A.

On the eighth day Dr. Bannerjee said to us that he did not feel there was any more hope for her recovery. She had said to my father before the operation that she did not wish to be kept alive by unnatural means. We agreed that she be taken off the respirator.

After that it was quick—for about twenty minutes the readout for her blood pressure gradually became lower, like some perverse basketball game. 80 over 30, 59 over 25, 57 over something, 40 over. . . . We called the minister, the one with the jokes who had often had lunch or breakfast with us at the hospital, but he wasn't in. I left a message.

Finally it was over. I hadn't realized that the monitor had been beeping with her heart—the darkness had hidden the sound from me. Now its stitching healed and held no spaces. It's odd that the obliteration of silence should stand for death. My father and I cried, awkwardly holding each other. I touched her forehead a last time—it already seemed cold to me—and I tried to close her eyes. I did not look back at her to see if they had closed; I was afraid they would stay open. We shook hands with Joe and with the doctor as we left.

My father seemed more comfortable with the events of the next few days. Even the bizarre experience of choosing a casket in the basement of the funeral parlor seemed routine to him. He casually pointed out one in some highly finished fruitwood, rose or cherry, I've already forgotten, that he said he would like for himself. There was a visitation the night before the funeral—there was no food or drink, but many people, ghosts of my childhood, appeared, and, gripping my hand in theirs, would tell me stories about me as a child, about my mother. In these stories, it seemed,

I was often the source of some mild mischief; and my mother, who, during all my school days worked in the bank, always dressed impeccably, represented order and decorum. In one, and this was recalled by several of her former colleagues, I had come to the bank with my dog, an overlarge shepherd named Captain. After visiting with my mother, I left by the side door, forgetting about the dog waiting at the front door. The dog became impatient and barked angrily at each person coming out of the bank. At the center of the stories was the picture of my mother trying to order the dog, nearly as large as she was, to go home. "Go home, Captain." Of course, the dog would not budge. I had to be called to retrieve him. This picture of my mother, who was not known for assertiveness, confronting the barking Captain, who was probably better known in the town than she, famous, among other things, for Friday-night dogfights on the lighted football field before the high-school games began—this dramatic and comic standoff intrigued my mother's friends. She had, I think, laughed about it at the time. Each story contained the dialogue, as if it were a gem of wisdom, "Go home, Captain." All night I listened to such stories, took hands, shook hands, and they were, for the most part, old hands, gnarled, the veins twisting futilely under thin worn skin.

The evening before the visitation, there was a knock at the door, and I answered because my father was on the phone—he was continually thinking of new calls to make. It was as if my mother's death was a gift, and it was his duty to give it to everyone she had known. The man at the door was bulky and tall, and I let him into the living room, where we sat in silence until my father came into the room. Although he hadn't identified himself, it became clear to me that he was a minister. He seemed at ease, almost enjoying himself, his large hands resting on his knees. His feet were enormous. My father seemed in awe of him—he told me afterward that the man had been the pastor of his mother's, my grandmother's, church. When the time came for prayer, he prayed eloquently—the man was an artist of prayer. His prayer was like a sax solo deep into a set when the players have cut through everything superfluous, body, instrument, listeners, and only the music remains, and something that lurks under music, at that. The old man prayed, and his voice was resonant and sad, but his heart was happy. Then, as he left, he said that it was my mother's cast-off remnant that we would be burying. I tried to think of her without her body, but she was gone, she had vanished the way the prayer vanished, the way music vanishes.

The joking minister presided over the funeral, and while his voice broke several times, showing real emotion, his oration was almost silly—what can you say about a woman who was quiet, who kept to herself, who was shy, a little hard of hearing, whose life was dedicated to finding enough patience to endure my father. . . . This said, or not said, the procession began to a little cemetery in the town, forty miles away, where my mother was born. This was her journey in life, from one little town to another, then back.

The procession stopped once at a rest area so the pallbearers, all elderly men, could relieve their bladders. The funeral director went from car to car, explaining and apologizing.

"We don't usually stop a funeral procession, but the pallbearers are so old. . . ." He grinned and shrugged.

It was cold at graveside, and the ground was uneven. A canvas cover had been pitched because the weather was darkening. After a final prayer, everyone went their own way. My father went with some of my mother's relatives, and I began the drive back to Nashville, since the forty-mile trip to the cemetery had been in that direction. It grew dark within an hour, and soon it began to rain in torrents. After seven hours of driving in one hideous downpour after another, I arrived home and fell exhausted into bed.

The first time I took Anna to my home town, I drove her along the back road that makes a shortcut from the interstate, the same one I took the day of the birds. She was charmed by the way it twisted through hills crowded with overhanging trees, by the old white clapboard Baptist church, and by the row of trees on the horizon, just before town, chewed into a kind of Pines of Rome, Appian Way topiary by grazing cattle. I don't know what she thought about the town, having grown up in a large city.

Small towns—other small towns, I suppose—seem ugly and stifling to me. I have forgotten myself that I was a child, and that children are so small. It was always a shock for me to walk into the door of my old house and be greeted by my mother and my father—to realize that I was not the kid who once got lost less than a block away while collecting newspapers and magazines for the Boy Scouts—after the Baptist church, the houses seemed to me endless, with their dark parlorways and little old ladies coming slowly to the door, dank smells drifting out to the porch where I waited, becoming more and more unsettled, until I didn't even remember which door I had knocked on last—after I had greeted my parents, and it never seemed to them any remarkable thing (as it did to me) that I was coming in the door, I had to will myself out of that childhood, remember that I was some kind of adult, grown up, back from the world for a moment. But soon that effort faded, and I was a kid again, or something close to it, sitting in the living room with my mother and Anna and the family album. Anna seemed to enjoy, no, to tolerate this ritual. My father disappeared to his basement workshop, a place where Anna would have been more at home than the living room. But we stayed, the three of us, my mother presiding, leafing the pages. I am the subject of this perusal, the baby me, the child me, my tricycles, my dogs. Here I am again, just before the pages where the smiles become self-conscious and then the pictures disappear entirely—me, arms akimbo, nine or ten years old, in my swimsuit in a vacation snapshot with a sun-browned friend I can almost remember. It was not difficult to be a child when there were other children to emulate.

Anna smiles and strokes my arm. No one asks her about her childhood. In this ceremony my mother is a merchant displaying not her wares but her world. Anna is her customer. Customers do not have lives. I am a child, almost a ghost in this transaction, yet it is my pictures she shows, pictures of my childhood.

My mother was one of five—not even the youngest, but the shyest. Her brothers will tell a story of how she spoke up at the table, asking for the last pork chop, the one destined for the plate of her father, old Doctor Jones, who began his second family when he was sixty. It might have been the only time she misbehaved at table. She wrote to her mother once a week until the old woman died in her late eighties. I see her always waiting or turning pages. Turning the pages of the album, as she does now, or the pages of some historical romance. Waiting with me for my father—he is late for supper, he is late for lunch, he has gone out for milk and must have found someone to talk to, he has stopped the car to run into a shop and now does not come out. . . . I see my mother fishing, sitting in a rowboat with a can of minnows, smoking one of the cigarettes that killed first her younger sister and then her. We would drive across pastures to find our fishing places, me sitting on the fender of the car, jumping off to open gates, watching the grasshoppers flare out in front of us. My mother is fishing for crappie—small perch-like speckled fish which tend to school in deep water. A red-and-white plastic bobber, a small lead sinker, the minnow hooked either through the lips or in the back under the dorsal fin. Then she sits smoking while small waves lap up against the sides of the rowboat. Brush and trees crowd down to the shore of the lake and overhang. Bullfrogs chug from the shadows. A whippoorwill, small and invisible, the plainest of birds, sings, amplified by the growing twilight. My mother is not really waiting for anything to happen. She enjoys catching the fish, but she is happy in this place, occasionally checking to see if her minnow has escaped. She does not think, I believe. She does not worry about her life, about me, her son, catching frogs and turtles at the far end of the lake. She and my father are sharing a moment of suspension. All conflicts, even the greatest, have time outs. When I return, I will tell her about the snakes I saw, the adventures I almost had, and she will pretend to listen. Something every mother has done.

The next time we visit, and the next, the album ritual is played out. Then Anna takes her tolerance to the basement, where an ossuary of walnut furniture competes with an enormous dismantled rug loom and with sections of a wrought-iron fence my father has scavenged from an abandoned cemetery, looking for all the world like train tracks at the bottom of a toy box. My father sands and glues in silence. I can love him like this, purpose turned to an end I can understand, his silence a blessing I think Anna can appreciate, even if it is only a kind of charging of energy for the next outburst.

One night, in our upstairs bedroom, I lose my temper and

throw a book, which strikes the door. My father appears at the bottom of the stairs. "Is everything all right?" he asks.

Like my mother, Anna made things right. She cowered before my anger, gave it its honor, shaped it like a pillar of flame before my eyes. How could I be the next thing which comes after a child without my father's example?

Here is a scene which never took place, which could never take place. I imagine it because it touches that vein of silence my mother always guarded, and Anna, too.

My mother is ironing. Anna is washing dishes. My mother would do the two things at the same time if she could. My father and I have gone on an errand, perhaps to renew a running argument with a tradesperson.

"How are things between you and James?" my mother asks, professionally nosing her iron into crevices and pleats—she could easily have steered the Titanic away from that iceberg.

"James is so much like his father," Anna says, squeaking a glass.

"Yes, they're a pair of pigs," my mother snorts.

"Grunting, feet in the trough, always at home in a crowd . . . ," perhaps Anna should say.

It's not that Anna and my mother had no conversations at all. It is just that my mother never in her life steered into an iceberg. She was on alert. Her motto was: stay close to the burrow, watch for owls, for the dog, the fox, the weasel, for bad weather, for quarry trucks at the crossings.

Life, and what is left of it in the mind, is like that toy chest, layers of parts and pieces piled and forgotten. Some scenes are lost, some simply inaccessible. The famous olfactory clue will often get you to the bottom, but it's a chance gift, and the human nose is vestigial, an artifact. It's sound for me, music, that pulls me into the lost places of my life, the gardens grown over, where doors are locked, boarded. I listened countless times to the Raag Yaman the week my mother died, driving the few miles from the hospital to our house to take a nap, or to the other side of town where the highway sighs like a zipper through enormous black-top parking lots, K-Mart and Safeway pushing the pigs and cows, the wheat, corn, and soybeans, miles farther from the town center. On my way to buy TV dinners or another pint of Black Jack I listened to the magic flute of Pannalal Ghosh.

I cannot make my mother speak to Anna, but I have perfect recall of the record jacket. "The usual practice is to expound this Raga in the evening or early part of the night. It creates a very quiet and subdued atmosphere and is very serene in character."

Now this listening, which I do in a kind of continuum, the tape resuming the moment I turn the ignition, is not really serene for me. I have moved from the crypt-like shadowed beeping of the ICU—this is what it must be like to be trapped inside a digital watch—to the world, bright sun, or God's dozen varieties of downpour. . . . The Raag Yaman takes me to our last summer in Toronto.

Anna and I were teetering, I suppose. It was a welcome thing for us to be spending the summer with Anna's friend Sanjiv and his sisters. I was attempting to make the Indian bamboo flutes then, and I was taking drumming lessons along with Sanjiv. I could sing the drumming patterns in a rapid singsong, a kind of rhythmic solfège called solkatu. "Ta din din na . . ." I still play the drumming exercises on my desk, on the sides of the refrigerator. I gave my drum, the two-headed mrdangam, made of jackwood and buffalo hide, to a drummer in Nashville who used to improvise with me. I wish now I had kept it, so I could sit down cross-legged in the middle of the floor and bang away until my palms stung, the feeling like the vibrations of a struck gong, subsiding but never quite disappearing. Anna and I were teetering in the balance of our lives together, and we were stumbling on the roots of Indian culture. When do we eat, what do we eat, how loud do we speak, who cleans the house. . . . It was a wonderful thicket for a man to hide from responsibility in. I played the raga Yaman for hours behind the closed door of our room while Anna read or washed dishes or dusted. I was past thinking—my mind was covered in the fallen shapes of the raga, like leaves, or better, snow—everything recognizable was smoothed, obliterated. I wanted to make it rain, to bring light out of darkness, and then see the darkness that lived between the pieces of the light. So I fell instead into bed with Kalika, Sanjiv's sister, and, after that disaster, with Sanjiv's blessing kept it all from Anna. There were words, rapid words, like the drumming syllables, between Sanjiv and Kalika, and Sanjiv fell on the stairs, and the next day Anna and I left and drove south toward Missouri. And when we arrived, it was high August, the tree crickets and cicadas put my drumming to shame, and there was nothing for us to talk about. We were two large blundering people escaped from a fine prison. Endless fields of corn, almost black, shimmered in the heat. We could feel ourselves growing coarser, enormous.

So with nothing to talk about, we talked about death. Anna's father had died some years before. Her mother had divorced him before that, and his non-existence in her family's mythology was only slightly disturbed by the actual event of his death. Anna and I had identified the body, signed the papers for cremation, driven home, and resumed our lives. Now we were reading together in the too-small walnut antique bed upstairs in my parents' house, and I had laid down my book. Thomas Mann in those days. The train lost, a single sentence driving me into my own snares.

"Why does my father behave like the grand inquisitor in restaurants? He has known some of these people since they were children."

"It's an inferiority complex."

"It's not complex. It's simple. It's a gift we give him. We should kick his ass, haul him out by his ears. . . . I should. Is that it? Is that what I have to do? I won't. You wouldn't."

"Wouldn't what?"

"You wouldn't even acknowledge your father. Even after he died."

"He made a mess of our lives."

"And your mother an accomplice . . . you an accomplice. You have an obligation to denounce him. If you refuse . . ."

"What am I refusing? He's dead. The world's without him. I don't have to suffer. I can choose not to remember him. He's dead. Think about it. Think about what that means."

"Then what can I do?" And I threw my book at the door.

No, nothing is the matter. I told Anna later that night about what had happened the week before with Kalika, and she listened, nodding. She was not angry. It was understandable, she said . . .

she and I had somehow been put off from each other. And I asked why was that. She shook her head and patted my hand, my arm. She didn't know. Such a thing could happen, an accident, like Sanjiv falling on the stairs. He wasn't hurt. He could have been killed, but he wasn't. We could choose not to be hurt. There she was, choosing again. In a short time we weren't together anymore. But my parents would be together always. This seemed better to me. For worse. But always. Not choosing. Where does all this choosing get you?

Sometimes I'd get my mother on the phone.

"How are things going? How is he?"

"He's better. He's not yelling. But he won't get the things I ask for."

"Then you should shop yourself. You know how to drive."

"He's always using the little car. He got it for me, but he's always driving it."

"Then use the other."

"It's too big."

I am a coward. Anna is a coward. My mother is a coward. We do not have the courage to change the world. We do not believe the world can be changed. Yet we leave the world—my mother has just performed this miracle—so it must be possible that the world can change a little.

It's early afternoon when I wake up. The rain has stopped, and new weather has moved in from the west. Sunlight is clamoring in from that side of the house, shaped and juggled by dancing trees. The house is dusty and mail is piled over the table like a landfill, but the room is still beautiful. Every speck of dust is rising and dancing in the light, nothing is falling. I have brought the flute I made in the basement of my parents' home. I take it and sit down in the middle of the moving light.

I can hear the drone, the tambura, and for a long while I sit and watch the dust become the tambura and the tambura become the dust. But because the flute is in my hands, and its sound is in my mind, like this language which means nothing until it is taken in,

I raise it to my lips and play. I can imagine that this is like the music I have been listening to for the past week, for half of my life, and for a while I do, knowing exactly where the raggedy record jackets of Pannalal Ghosh are filed, between the Japanese and the Irish albums. "The Gramophone Company of India (Private) Limited. Dum Dum. India." But after a while I begin to listen to what I am playing. The sound is scratchy, airy, like the edges of far clouds that tend to dissolve when you watch them closely. But the pitch inside, the crying, for that is what it is, is telling me a story. When I was a child of three and four, I would lie in bed at night and tell myself stories. They could not have been long stories, because children fall asleep quickly, nor did the stories have much of a plot—"A little boy went for a walk in the woods until he was lost. . . ." This was, then, the story in the flute playing, a little story like that. And I won't say what it said to me, because I can't exactly. I can't say whether the rain came when the child bid it, whether the child came home or disappeared over the mountains. I will say that I played a while longer, and put the flute down in my lap, and listened to that droning in my head that was the dust, not crying, because of the listening, and then I put the flute away, and I doubt that I shall ever need to play it again.

There was a time, during the rain, that made of those last few days a kind of single dusk, when we were all so worn down, so tortured and defeated by hoping, that death began to seem less terrible—I was alone with my mother in the ICU. My father had gone home for a nap. Joe was reading, studying for a course that would advance his career, perhaps send him to a hospital in a city where the ICU would never be this quiet. I saw her move her arm, and I went over to the bed. She seemed awake and was looking at me intently, her brow furrowed. It seemed almost a question, but it might have been the intensity of her gaze. She was seeing me, and the rocking of the ventilator, filling her lungs and releasing, in that constant hissing and clicking rhythm, like waves nudging a boat, did not seem to distract her concentration.

I took her hand and said, "I love you." And though she had never done this before, she squeezed my hand and held it tightly. It must have been an enormous exertion for her. Then her hand relaxed but her expression did not change. She continued looking at me and her frown, if anything, deepened.

"I know," I said, and her frown gradually disappeared, and the light in her eyes, and I could see her falling far away while the ventilator continued to rock her body. "I know," I said again.

There was a time when they rose from a tree. Before, the darkness had been a long time lying on them, then the trees were standing there. They had not been there in the darkness, there had been nothing at all, but now the trees were becoming and they felt it. There was not just one tree now, but a forest of trees, and they rose from the trees and settled again because there was too much to pull up. They were all the same somehow, and some not yet ready. They rose and settled for some time, and the din, they were all crying out to each other, had risen already—it was a wrenching but a certain thing and finally they rose high enough to circle around and see they were whole in the air. And they made the shape that fills and spills out again and they cried out to each other and they almost settled into the trees again like a rock in water but the wind came across the far fields and it was hard enough to rise on and they made the shape that sees the sun and holds the land above, the shape that spins the world, the shape that grows the world bigger and the sky always asking for them. And their hearts grew warm as if they might burst and they toiled and they fell and rose again and their hearts kept filling as they made the shape that sees all things—

And in darkness or light when you cannot speak, and have given up speaking, and when the pain has become as far away as the earth, you can grow small, so small no one can see you, and there is nothing down below you, not darkness, not light, not the flat green suffering world—and you are not flying, but what else could you call it?

Listening
to Mozart

Buffalo, 1969

━━━━━━

When I was discharged from the service, I called
or wrote everybody I could think of who had anything to do with
music. Within a week I had been offered a position with a New
Music group at the State University of New York in Buffalo. I
didn't imagine I had especially good luck. I just supposed there
would be something for me to do, and in the presence of such
powerful innocence, all obstacles fell away. The Vietnam War was
still going strong, and I was needed to fill in for an unlucky
fluteplayer whose reserve unit had been called up. I think I was
less hostile to New Music than most of the musicians I knew in

those days, but my notion of it probably wasn't much different. Many of my teachers hadn't even acknowledged its existence. At student recitals, the director of my music school would grouse and grumble under his breath if he heard even Prokofiev. To me, New Music was the refuge of intellectual oddballs, from Charles Ives to John Cage. No tunes, difficult notation, perverse rhythms, atonality—we called it blip-blop music. I knew and genuinely liked a few pieces by Schoenberg, Berg, and Webern, even Berio and Varese. I had even spent a summer at Aspen working on a fiendishly difficult piece for flute and piano by Pierre Boulez, but I really didn't know what I'd be getting into. However, after all that marching and standing inspection, after all those orders and ridiculous short haircuts, I wasn't inclined to be too particular about civilian life.

I picked the straightest road to Buffalo from Washington, D.C., that I could find on the map. My heater wasn't working very well, so I had to stop every hour or so and drink coffee until my feet thawed out. The road didn't exactly turn out to be a major throughway and certainly wasn't straight, but there were a lot of little towns with warm cafés along the way. After a while the road got straighter and the land got flatter, but by then it had begun to snow. Just when my feet were starting to get used to the cold, I couldn't tell where the road was anymore—everything was flat and white. I tried to imagine myself somewhere else, like the early-morning fishing trips I used to go on with my father. We'd get up early, have flapjacks and coffee before sunrise in some little joint like the places where I'd been stopping to warm my feet—I'd have been sleepy, but filled with excitement and anticipation. I loved to watch the sun rise—it was almost my favorite game, to try to see that molten rind of light when it first popped up on the horizon. It *had* been fun, going fishing, at least until we got where we were going.

So there I was, peering into the snow, thinking about how seldom anything had ever come of my expectations, how big and gray those lakes and rivers had been, and how seemingly empty. It was not easy to daydream, because the car kept fishtailing. I had about given up on seeing the road again when a snowplow materialized in front of me and I followed him nearly the rest of the way to Buffalo. Behind us the wide fields, empty and white, closed over with blowing snow, and the windshield wiper on the passenger side of my old green Rambler squeaked once and died. The light inside the car became more peaceful as half the windshield snowed over.

In Buffalo the sun was shining on fresh snowdrifts, and everything was plowed in neat, sharp edges. I was to spend the first few days, until I could find a place to rent, at the house of one of the composers, a Frenchman with scarcely more English than I had French, Jean Claude or Jean Paul or Jean Jean (no, Jeanjean was a composer of flute études). He quickly lost interest in attempting conversation with me and returned to his study, where he composed with the aid of a protractor and tables of logarithms. His house was large and old. If I touched anything anywhere, a magazine slid to the floor. I wanted to use the telephone, but a woman in a hidden room somewhere was on the line. Someone showed me to my room. I went to the bathroom. Became lost. Found my room again, and slept. I dreamt I was fishing with many others on the banks of a large river. Everyone was pulling in fish but me. Somehow I could see the fish swimming in the river, near the bottom, their tails sweeping grandly. A woman speaking gibberish into a telephone accompanied my sleep. When I woke it was almost dark, and my heart, it was, how do you say, almost dark as a well—I was still half-dreaming, with a cartoon French accent— I sat at the foot of the stairs and telephoned my parents. I had promised my mother I would call so she wouldn't have to worry. My father answered the phone. I told him I was fine and that there was a lot of snow, that I was going to have to replace a windshield wiper. We were able to talk about windshield wipers for quite some time. When my mother got on the line I could tell she was pleased that I had had such a good talk with my father.

The next morning my first rehearsal was of a piece involving only a few other instruments and which for me consisted almost entirely of sustained pianissimo notes in the five ledger line range. This, I must explain, is difficult, even with trick fingerings and much pinching and squeezing of the lips. It is not unusual for a headache to result from such straining. The composer conducted. He kept asking, "Is it possible? Is it possible?" I reassured him. I understood. He *wanted* those high notes to sound painful. It was masterful. The *sound* of pain.

I met Alice in the office. I can usually tell a woman who has aspirin. Perhaps this is foolish. Perhaps all women keep aspirin as a method of introduction, a ploy passed on from mothers to daughters. Only a sensitive man would have a headache. Alice directed me to my next rehearsal. Gray eyes, a long blond braid. She was an assistant administrator, the person responsible for distributing my rehearsal assignments, even my paycheck. She was rather pretty in an unfocused sort of way.

"I hear you're staying with Jean Paul. You must be starved. He doesn't keep anything but cat food in the house. Would you like to come over to my place this evening for dinner?"

I accepted her invitation gratefully, and I had begun the groundwork in my mind for something clever about Jean Paul's crowded and dilapidated house, but I was too slow at it, for Alice suddenly bustled off and left me in mid-mumble.

When I was in the seventh grade, my father found me a flute teacher in a nearby city. He had been recommended to us by the man who had already sold us several flutes, the proprietor of George's Music Store. This store was rather distant from our home town, but my father was very much at home in mercantile affairs and willing to drive the extra mile for a good deal. He and George had struck several arcane bargains over these flutes, and consequently my father trusted his musical judgment. The teacher's name was Lawrence Flowers. He was supposed to be a fine teacher but very demanding of his students. His method of teaching was simple. He gave me a difficult Bach sonata to practice. When I came for my next lesson, it was soon evident that I could not play the rhythms. I had never been taught to count. Mr. Flowers told me that if I could not play the rhythms correctly by the next lesson, he would take the music away and give me something simpler. I went home and learned to count. I understand now how I was motivated, but I do not understand how

I learned. I suppose I stared at the music until I was struck with knowledge. It has not happened with me or any of my students since. It was, apparently, the exclusive genius of Mr. Flowers to teach in such an economical manner.

Later he played a recording of the Mozart Flute Concerto in D Major for me. It was a recording of L'Orchestre de la Suisse Romande conducted by Ernest Ansermet. The flutist, whose name I don't recall, did not play with virtuosity, but with simplicity. His playing did not call attention to itself. It was so self-effacing, there was nothing there but the music. I did not think this at the time, of course. I had never heard a flute concerto. I had never heard Mozart. I was thrilled. There was a moment in the slow movement which was so exquisitely beautiful that I thought my heart would break. Later I learned that this was a German sixth chord, resolving under the sustained flute, holding the fifth degree of the scale, the dominant; that Mozart had originally written this concerto in another key for the oboe, that he had transposed it up a step and sold it to an amateur flutist to make a quick buck. He was in turn cheated by the flutist. But that day, sitting next to Mr. Flowers, I experienced only the wonder of Mozart, and decided that I could have no higher aspiration than to perform his concerto.

Alice, I learned, was a soprano and had gone to school in Philadelphia at the same time I had. She had studied with the same woman who taught voice at my school, Madame Lavalle, a teacher with an international reputation. Alice's career plans were confused, however; her parents had been killed in an automobile crash only a year before, and this was their house, the house Alice grew up in. I had been completely intimidated when I drove into the neighborhood. I was sure I had the wrong address.

"In summer, there are pheasants wandering in the back yards," Alice said, pouring some of the cheap wine I brought. "The gardens are beautiful. But you wait too long for spring. Do you know that, downtown, there are ropes along the sidewalks for people to hold on to, to keep from being blown over by the wind?"

I told her something about winters in Missouri, a version of my snag-a-cow-fallen-through-the-ice-fishing-in-spring story.

"Do you remember playing *Lucia di Lamermoor* in Philadelphia? I heard you play the Mad Scene duet with Anna Moffo. It was wonderful. How did you rehearse with her?"

I told her that in those days every opera I played I was playing for the first time; and that consequently my mental state often teetered between smug arrogance and sheer terror. I hadn't known what to expect—I was called to Miss Moffo's dressing room by a stage manager who refused to speak English; that she, however, had been gracious; and that she sang the cadenza exactly the same each time. There was no problem in playing it perfectly, even from the distance of the pit to center stage.

Then two of the sopranos at school had become interested in the role and asked me to play the cadenza with them for their lessons. They were not so steady.

"Sometimes they left out notes, sometimes they added notes. I had to guess. When I performed it, I hadn't realized the pitfalls. It's exciting enough without the surprises."

"But then what is the point of it?" Alice asked.

"What do you mean?"

"If you don't change it, if you don't make something different of it, something, I don't know . . . personal, what's the point of being a singer?"

"It's like a game with rules, I guess. If you don't like the rules, you can always write music of your own. Or just do something else. Besides, your voice, just the sound of your voice . . . what could be more personal than that?"

I suppose Alice and I were both nervous. She kept getting up to do something in the kitchen, then returning and sitting down. She was in the next room when I began talking about Quantz calling Italian singers fantastic dunces. I realized that she probably couldn't hear me when she came to the door.

"Come in here, James, I'd like you to meet somebody."

I went into the kitchen, and there was a big green-and-yellow parrot in a cage on the counter.

"This is Max. Max, I want you to meet James."

Max gave me a sharp look and ambled over to the far side of his cage.

"I've had Max for six months. I'm teaching him to sing Cherubino's aria, 'Non so piu,' from *Figaro*."

"This I'd like to hear."

Alice coaxed and sang to Max for quite some time, but he merely shifted from one foot to the other and watched her carefully.

I began to feel a little uncomfortable and tried to distract her. "Perhaps he'd rather do Papageno. Or Papagena. Or both."

Alice was flushed with effort. "I know. This always works."

She picked up the cage and began walking from room to room, all the while singing, "Non so piu, cosa son, cosa faccio, or di foco ora sono di ghiaccio . . ."

By the time she had made her first circuit and come back through the kitchen, Max was a different bird. His pupils were dilating and contracting like a berserk camera lens. And he was making little chortling noises in his throat.

When Alice started through the house the second time I noticed the door to Max's cage was open, swinging in time to Mozart. I was just wondering to myself how I was going to tell if it was Alice or the bird singing from the next room when there was a piercing scream. I ran into the dining room, then the living room. There was another scream. In a kind of den-library I found Alice. The cage was on its side on the floor and Max was perched on her shoulder pulling beakfuls of hair from her head.

"Please get him off me. Get him OFF me," she pleaded.

When I got closer I could see that Max was using his beak and sometimes even a foot to pull at Alice's gradually unraveling hair. Perhaps he saw her braid as a puzzle, a knot to untie, some kind of challenge to his considerable intelligence. Her hair really was her finest feature, and Max was getting big hanks of it. He was proceeding rather methodically, and it seemed to me he was really enjoying himself. Alice had given up swatting at him but continued to whimper imploringly. I had to fight against a sudden impulse to bolt and let the two of them work things out.

"Please, James."

All right. I would do something. I thrust my hand in front of Max, about chest high, or breastbone high. We had had a budgie, a parakeet, when I was a kid, and that was the way you got him to sit on your finger.

"Here, Max. Climb up."

Max stopped pulling Alice's hair and gave me a bright look. He looked at my hand. Just as I realized he wasn't going to climb aboard, he bit me hard.

"Damn it. He bit me. And I'm bleeding," I announced, almost relieved to be more fully included in the reality of the proceedings.

"Get the cage! Get the cage!" Max had gone back to pulling Alice's hair.

I picked up the cage and held it as close to Max as I could, at the same time trying to keep as far on its other side as possible, after the manner of Clyde Beatty and his chair.

Max coolly hopped on the cage, pulled himself around to the open door by grabbing the bars with his beak, and climbed up to his perch, seeming quite pleased with himself.

"He seems to think of himself as more the Queen of the Night type, I think."

Alice had gone to get me a bandage and did not reply.

Alice gave me a bottle of red wine to open, and while I struggled with it, served our overcooked pasta. The wine, however, was good, better probably than I'd ever had before. We ate for a while in a kind of relieved silence.

"I'm really sorry. He's never done anything like that before. It must be the excitement. Maybe he doesn't like you."

"Maybe he doesn't like Mozart."

Alice didn't laugh.

"That was supposed to be funny."

"Oh, I'm sorry."

She looked at me a little sideways and I was reminded fleetingly of Max.

"I'm psychic, you know," she said, taking my hand and glancing briefly at my palm as if it were, I don't know, a weather report. "There's somebody else in your life. Waiting, I think. But you've got plenty of time. You're not very good with birds, either, are you?"

Nobody waits in this world, I thought.

"I don't think we should make love this time," she said quietly. "But next time would be fine."

In the fifth grade, I chose the flute to play in the school band. I had been told by my parents I could not play the instrument which had been recommended by the band director, the French horn, because it was too expensive. My parents suggested the trumpet or the clarinet. But I recall when, as a fourth-grader, I first saw, close up, a flute in the hands of a fifth-grade band student. It was that bright nickel-silver color, and the mouthpiece was so odd. It seemed to me at once more mystical and more mechanically interesting than the other instruments.

Having chosen the flute, I discovered that I could not play it. My father could produce a sound easily, but it was not in his temperament to show me how he did it. Instead, he made jokes about my ineptitude. We kept the flute hidden in the linen closet. It was rented but would have cost $140 if it were stolen by roaming gangs of flute thieves. Finally the band teacher showed me how to hold the thing and how to produce a sound. More than the sound it made, which I thought was rather ordinary, I liked the feeling of pressing down the keys against the subtle resistance of their springs. And it was a handsome sight, bright and silvery in its case, shining against a background of dark blue velvet.

The next day Alice was distant and official, providing me with a schedule of rehearsals and conferences leading up to a concert at the Art Museum in a few weeks. I rented a room several blocks from the University, and for a week I was too busy to think about anything but music. I went to sleep at night with my lips swollen and woke in the morning with my neck and fingers stiff.

Whatever plan existed for the concerts and rehearsals came from some remote bureaucratic distance. Compositions which required a conductor (most did, even those utilizing relatively small forces, because of the complexity of the music) were conducted by their composers. If a composer was not present, another composer would try his hand. These chaps were all in the same boat together, and realized probably that times might not always be as magnanimous, as propitious as these for the experimental, the difficult, and the downright repulsive. They endured each other's music with a stiff upper lip, which only occasionally revealed the sneer hiding behind.

On the other hand, some of the music in which I was involved could be managed without a conductor. There was a trio with piano and cello in which I was required to sing and play in octaves with myself. This was a difficult process which necessitated much individual practice and a nasty vibrating feeling in my head when the voice pitches and flute pitches were out of phase. Another piece, a kind of New Music golden oldie, was the "Sequenza" for solo flute by Luciano Berio. I was pleased to be asked to play something which I already knew, one which I was fairly certain would seem flashy enough to stir up a little applause. An unrelenting cascade of swirling and stuttering notes, the piece is surprisingly effective, even with unsophisticated audiences. There was not time, nor did I have the inclination, to memorize it, and page turning would have been impossible. The music opened like a roadmap and was propped up on two music stands. Some pieces required three or even four stands. The lengthy horizontal scroll of music was very much an emblem of the kind of music we were playing, functional in a sense (page-turners seldom were equal to the complexities of the notation), but also an important element of the style, like a baseball player's chewing tobacco. I decided to play the "Sequenza" on my alto flute. This, while more difficult, gave the piece a more distant color, and allowed me more freedom with contrasts of volume.

I sometimes saw Alice hurrying down the hallways, her braid bouncing behind her. I remember thinking that Max couldn't have managed to create *all* that awkwardness between us.

There was an oboe player named Fred Small who played on one of the larger pieces we were rehearsing. His specialty, I learned, was multiphonics. Multiphonics are chords, groups of notes sounded simultaneously, and it's possible to produce them on single-line instruments like the oboe or flute. The individual notes in the chords sometimes have quarter-tone or even eighth-tone relationships to each other, so the effect of the chord is often peculiar, sometimes shimmering, sometimes strident. My own impression is that they often sound like the screeching of metal on metal, a locomotive with wheels locked after someone has pulled the emergency cord. On a considerably smaller scale, of course. Freddy had written a book on the subject. He was always suggesting fingerings to me which he was sure would extract sounds from my flute capable of transforming lead into gold. After I had huffed and puffed, and spit on my music for a while, he would pretend to give up on me. But he always came back with a new one.

I asked Freddy about Alice.

"Alice. That girl in the office or the bass clarinet player?"

"I don't know a bass clarinet player named Alice."

"Oh yeah, she's on leave this semester. You'd love her. When she puts that reed in her mouth and licks it, it's unbearable. She plays well, too."

"But what about Alice in the office?"

"Oh, her. Well, she's pretty spacey, don't you think?"

At the end of the rehearsal I went by the office and asked for Alice. The woman told me she hadn't been feeling well and had gone home early. I had the evening off, the first time since my duet with Max. I thought about calling, but I couldn't think what to say. If I just drove by, maybe I'd be inspired.

Alice's car was in the drive. It was extremely cold, and the wind was making drifts, changing its mind, and making new drifts. And then I was standing on her front porch, another of the world's undecided creatures.

I finally rang and Alice, wearing a white terry robe, let me in rather quickly.

"They told me you weren't feeling well. I thought I'd see if . . ."

She started to kiss me. I hadn't even taken off my coat. The door wasn't completely pushed shut. Little wisps of snow were still shooting in around our feet. I tried to manage all the stage business while maintaining that kiss. It was obviously supposed to be a long one. Finally I had the door closed and my coat un-zipped. Alice had come up for air and was holding me tightly under my coat. When I tried to lean in one direction or another she wouldn't budge. When I started to talk to her she would kiss me again. I don't know how long we were in the hall. It seemed like half an hour, but it was probably only a few minutes. Eventually I managed to get Alice a little off balance and half dragged, half waltzed her to her bedroom. When we got on the bed, Alice moaned, "We shouldn't, we shouldn't," and I attempted to pull away, only to have her pull me back with inhuman strength. Finally, almost apologetically, we made love.

Afterward, the quiet was oppressive. I noticed there was a clock with a lopsided tick in the hallway. Then I heard somebody singing "Non so piu" from another part of the house. Of course it was Max. It wasn't half bad. It really sounded like Alice, like a real person, but like a person who just wanted to sing the first measure over and over. His pitch was pretty good, too. Sometimes he'd make that noise that you hear in jungle movies. A kind of gargling sound. I guess it's regular parrot singing. Then he'd go back to Cherubino.

"The reason I got this stupid parrot . . ."

I realized that Alice was crying.

". . . Is that my mother had a parrot. I grew up with cats and a parrot. It could sing like Max. Better than Max. It ate at the table with the people. 'Polly wants a cracker or an apple.' That's what it would say and stare at the damn peas or whatever. You know, with its head cocked to one side and that stupid flashlight look in its eye. Then my mother would feed it with a spoon. Its cage was always full of food and the cats would come and steal from it. They'd reach through the bars with their paws. My mother loved that bird. But it was so mean to me. If I fell down and hurt myself and cried, Polly would cry, too. Mock me. It was infuriating."

Alice slid down so the cover was halfway over her head and I had to strain to hear her.

"One time I got it to call the cats. 'Call the cats, Polly. Kitty, kitty, kitty. Call the cats.' Polly was in a good mood and called the cats. I know I didn't leave the cage door open. The cats just did it themselves. Things like that happen . . . Max . . . Max knows I can't stand him."

Max gave us a few more fragments of Mozart and then kind of dried up. It was quiet again. I think I was thinking about two things at once, about the cats and the parrot, and about me, and where I was—I could see myself on Alice's front porch like a bear come in from the forest, and here I was, in her bed, and there was something about the parrot I was supposed to appreciate . . . and I think I must have fallen asleep. Then the clock struck and startled me, and I sat up in bed and I had the clearest picture of Anna, the last time I had seen her, before she went into the hospital, and we were sitting on the floor of her apartment and she was reciting, "And James was a very small snail." I could hear her voice. It did not seem such a bad thing to be a very small snail. Then I realized where I was, and I saw that Alice had gone to sleep, too. I kissed her on the forehead, but she didn't wake or stir. So I dressed and let myself out. There was a full moon harassed by clouds that might have been those same wisps of snow in the front hall. In the places where it had melted and refrozen, the crust of snow glowed warmly. Every shape was softened, but the sound of my feet on the snow was startlingly sharp. I wondered where the pheasants were.

After almost a year of little progress with the flute, I noticed a big chart on the band room wall with a list of students' names and lines of stars after the names. A kid told me you got a star for each hour you practiced. I decided I would like to have the longest line of stars after my name. I began to practice. Most of this effort resulted in an accumulation of bad habits which required years of progressively more expensive teachers to eliminate. It seemed to me at the time, however, that I was finally learning the flute. My tone was weak and breathy, but I could play all the notes in the chromatic scale. To prove it, my father taught me to play "Stardust" in one horrifying two-hour session in my bedroom. I remember that he whistled it for me, and I suspect that, like those Lucias that were to vex me later on, he may have occasionally changed a note, and then perversely changed it back, not so much to keep me on my toes, but innocently, out of his natural fund of inventiveness.

It was my plan to learn to play the other woodwind instruments, the clarinet, the oboe, and the bassoon. But first I would master the flute. And while I did take a few clarinet lessons, I never got past working at the flute. It was like some women I have known since, always holding something back, constantly breaking my heart. The clarinet was a disappointment, and I soon gave it up. I could make a pleasant tone from the beginning. But it was not difficult enough to interest me. You could always get a grip on it. Playing the flute, as a teacher of mine often told me (yet another Frenchman, a very old man, wrinkled and stooped), looking at me sadly with his bloodshot eyes, the smell of Pernod and stale pipe smoke on his breath, "Playing the flute eez like trying to hold a feesh."

The next day Freddy and I were rehearsing a scene from a chamber opera with a string quartet. A male and a female voice intoned loony non sequiturs about doorknobs and wallpaper while we held more impossibly long highnotes, especially chosen, it seemed, to create pain in the lips and cramps in the shoulders. Even Freddy was complaining.

" 'Pierrot' this ain't," he said wisely.

"Why are there such long gaps in the music with nothing happening?" I asked. "Is there another character?"

"No. I've done another piece like this. There's stuff on tape. They probably won't even play it before the performance. You're gonna love it."

Freddy gazed sadly at a row of reeds in a scuffed leather compact. "Doo-doo."

"What?" Then I realized the nature of his contemplation. "Oh, reeds."

"Doo-doo." This time with an air of finality. Freddy brightened. "So how are you doing with the lady of the office?"

"Like your reeds."

Freddy said nothing, produced a razor-sharp knife, and began vigorously scraping a reed, producing a sound not unlike a cat with a hairball.

The concert was well attended and had a genuine feeling of excitement. A lot of New Music concerts I had played in had seemed to me more like the clandestine meetings of an illegal secret society. These people seemed happy, expansive. Even the composers were bustling about, only a few of them surly. By intermission it was becoming apparent that the concert was a great success. Applause had been long and enthusiastic. I loved sitting on the stage. I could look out over the audience and see the tops of bare trees through huge glass walls. The lights of the city gave the night sky a lovely glow.

The second half began, or didn't begin, with a problem. The cellist who played in my singing piece had an attack of stomach flu or nerves and couldn't get out of the bathroom. It took another fifteen minutes before we were able to get on stage. He looked terribly pale. I had managed to croak through the simultaneous singing and playing section rather well, I thought, when the cellist dropped his bow. There were titters from the front row. If he hadn't made such a big deal of it, we could have gone on without breaking the mood. The audience never settled down after that. We were applauded mostly for effort.

Backstage, I noticed Alice. Since our night together we had avoided each other again. It had become almost a routine with us, tides or something. I was holding my alto flute when a stagehand called me. He didn't know how to set up the music stands for the Berio "Sequenza." There was Alice standing near us. I handed her my alto flute and went to adjust the music stands. After unfolding the music and balancing the stands, I went back to get my flute so the curtain could be opened and the piece begun. No Alice. No flute.

Why has she done this thing? My heart tightens in a spasm of—what, stage fright? For some reason, without my flute, I am helpless, foolish. This is all some kind of silly game with its bowing and applauding and patient listening. Alice has pulled away its mask. I feel almost like weeping.

There is a place, right under my breastbone, where I feel a kind of glowing pain. When I was a child, when I felt this, I would say my feelings were hurt. It's such an odd thing—that there is an actual, physical place in my chest I can feel hurting. Where has she gone? Why has she left me alone like this?

This is all a wave which washes over me and then retreats. I take a deep breath and the next wave is smaller, and is more like anger than anything else. I begin to pull myself together.

"Where is the blond woman holding my flute?" I ask in my most imperious, artistic voice.

I can hear that voice. Or something in it. It's a long time, years later, and Madame T., a grande dame of the keyboard, is announcing imperiously, "I won't go on stage until that person in the front row is removed from the hall. He has been fidgeting."

We're supposed to play the Brandenburg Concerto No. 5, and the violin soloist and I are standing together in the wings while the stage manager tries to placate the old bat. When she finally realizes he's not going to throw out a paying customer, she reluctantly agrees to go on stage. And the three of us, smiling warmly, stride into the lights. A few moments later, the violinist and I play our accompaniment figures so loudly during her harpsichord solo, she reddens and veins stand out in her forehead like caterpillars. She might have stroked out. Temperament is not without its risks.

But that evening in Buffalo, people were already scurrying about like roaches. There is always, apparently, a market for tyrants. There was a real problem, after all. Alice had disappeared, and so had my flute. A half-dozen people were wandering about backstage, calling her name. Someone was sent to scout out the women's rooms. I spread out my tails and sat down on the floor. Two hundred people were waiting to hear a solo flute piece performed, but I was no longer to be counted among them. I was thinking about how nice it would be to just get in my car and drive south until I could find some place where I could go fishing. I was trying to visualize those big fish fanning just above the bottom, when Freddy tapped me on the shoulder. He held the flute with two fingers, rather at a distance from himself, as if it were distasteful. Nasty metal thing with no reed.

"She was staring out the window in the stairwell at the trees. Said she had no idea you were supposed to be playing."

The curtain was opened, and I made my entrance. The applause seemed knowing, ironic, as if it were the voice of a living thing, something at the back of a dark cave. At this point it would not have surprised me if I had knocked over both music stands.

The rest of the concert unwound normally. In the final piece, the opera scene with the long-held woodwind notes, I began to notice the strain of the evening. My back ached. Freddy's briefcase containing his spare oboe was in the way of my left foot. I couldn't get comfortable in the chair. The doorknob-sprechstimme seemed more ridiculous than ever.

Then I discovered the opera's final ingredient. The taped sounds that filled in the gaps, that floated in and out of the room like a ghost. Mozart! It was cruel. Fragments of the piano concertos, of the violin sonatas. Blowing through the room like leaves. I looked over the audience through the glass wall at arthritic trees hunched against the blue night sky. Something in e minor (a blue color to me) floated by. Freddy kicked my foot. I was supposed to be playing. I took a deep breath and joined in the music-making.

I saw Alice again in the post-concert melee. It wasn't easy to get through the well-wishers, but I managed. She had on her coat and had almost slipped out the stage door.

"What happened with the flute?" I asked in what I hoped was my kindest tone.

"Oh, I just didn't realize you were about to play," she said brightly. Then, after a moment. "That Fred. That oboe player. He is a very rude person."

"I'm sorry, Alice," I said.

"It's all right, James," she said, and she patted my arm.

I thought she was going out the door, but instead she took my hand and led me to the stairwell.

"See what I was looking at."

There was a nice view of trees surrendering to the night, holding their arms up wearily.

"I was looking at them, too, during that last piece."

"I was thinking about you and Max. Well, really about me and Max. I don't know if I want to be a singer. You just repeat the same thing over and over. The only difference between me and Max is that he doesn't sing if he doesn't feel like it."

"Max doesn't know what he says when he says it."

"Do you really think they don't know what they're doing?"

"Who doesn't know?"

She shook her head. Then she took my hand, and I thought she was going to say something about parrot bites, but it was the weather report again.

"It's all changed. Your waiting time is up. And where Max bit you is all better." Then she kissed the place where the bird got me, like a good mother. She left me standing on the staircase. I even called after her, but she didn't turn around. I looked at the trees and wondered what in the world it was that musicians do and why, until a guy moving sound equipment bumped into me and broke the spell.

During the long intermission someone had given me a note about a phone call. I had answered an advertisement I saw pinned to the bulletin board a week earlier—flutist needed for a touring chamber orchestra. There would be some solo work involved. I had sent my resume. The conductor of the chamber orchestra wanted me to call him. The next day I called him and we arranged an audition. The only way we could get together was for me to meet him at the Detroit airport. I played for him in a conference room. He was rather pleasant in a grandfatherly kind of way. Pudgy, white hair, glasses fallen down on his nose, a bit of the scholar. I played both Mozart concertos for him. Execrably, it seemed to me. I was humiliated. It sounded so awful. I kept saying, "Is this enough?" And he kept saying, "No, I want to hear a little more." Until I had played through all the movements. Then he said he liked my playing and offered me the job on the spot. I could start in two months. We shook hands, and I wandered around the airport for a while, slightly dazed, watching the people, watching kids who didn't seem at all interested in airplanes landing and taking off. I made up my mind to call Anna. Hobbs would know where to find her. Then it was time for my flight back to Buffalo.

When I was fourteen I played a movement of a Mozart flute concerto at the state band contest. It was the one I first heard at my lesson with Mr. Flowers. I had won a blue ribbon, and I was walking home from the high school after the competition. There had been some rain earlier, and there were puddles on the sidewalk reflecting the scattered clouds and even me, a giant stepping over them. It was springtime, the lawns were a light green, bordered with daffodils, and there were new leaves on the trees. I remember jumping up and grabbing a leaf as I walked under a tree. I was walking down the nicest street in town, holding a maple leaf in my hand, and suddenly I could hear the slow movement of that Mozart concerto in my head. I dropped the leaf and stood still to listen. I can see myself, feel myself, under the maples and elms, standing in a sidewalk puddle. I could not see what was under its surface. When I looked down at it, even though I knew there was only wet sidewalk there, all I could see was the sky.

The Iowa Short Fiction Award and John Simmons Short Fiction Award Winners

1995
Listening to Mozart,
Charles Wyatt
Judge: Ethan Canin

1995
May You Live in Interesting Times, Tereze Glück
Judge: Ethan Canin

1994
The Good Doctor,
Susan Onthank Mates
Judge: Joy Williams

1994
Igloo among Palms,
Rod Val Moore
Judge: Joy Williams

1993
Happiness, Ann Harleman
Judge: Francine Prose

1993
Macauley's Thumb, Lex Williford
Judge: Francine Prose

1993
Where Love Leaves Us,
Renée Manfredi
Judge: Francine Prose

1992
My Body to You, Elizabeth Searle
Judge: James Salter

1992
Imaginary Men, Enid Shomer
Judge: James Salter

1991
The Ant Generator,
Elizabeth Harris
Judge: Marilynne Robinson

1991
Traps, Sondra Spatt Olsen
Judge: Marilynne Robinson

1990
A Hole in the Language,
Marly Swick
Judge: Jayne Anne Phillips

1989
Lent: The Slow Fast,
Starkey Flythe, Jr.
Judge: Gail Godwin

1989
Line of Fall, Miles Wilson
Judge: Gail Godwin

1988
The Long White,
Sharon Dilworth
Judge: Robert Stone

1988
The Venus Tree, Michael Pritchett
Judge: Robert Stone

1987
Fruit of the Month, Abby Frucht
Judge: Alison Lurie

1987
Star Game, Lucia Nevai
Judge: Alison Lurie

1986
Eminent Domain, Dan O'Brien
Judge: Iowa Writers' Workshop

1986
Resurrectionists,
Russell Working
Judge: Tobias Wolff

1985
Dancing in the Movies,
Robert Boswell
Judge: Tim O'Brien

1984
Old Wives' Tales,
Susan M. Dodd
Judge: Frederick Busch

1983
Heart Failure, Ivy Goodman
Judge: Alice Adams

1982
Shiny Objects, Dianne Benedict
Judge: Raymond Carver

1981
The Phototropic Woman,
Annabel Thomas
Judge: Doris Grumbach

1980
Impossible Appetites,
James Fetler
Judge: Francine du Plessix Gray

1979
Fly Away Home, Mary Hedin
Judge: John Gardner

1978
A Nest of Hooks, Lon Otto
Judge: Stanley Elkin

1977
The Women in the Mirror,
Pat Carr
Judge: Leonard Michaels

1976
The Black Velvet Girl,
C. E. Poverman
Judge: Donald Barthelme

1975
*Harry Belten and the
Mendelssohn Violin Concerto,*
Barry Targan
Judge: George P. Garrett

1974
*After the First Death There Is
No Other,* Natalie L. M. Petesch
Judge: William H. Gass

1973
The Itinerary of Beggars,
H. E. Francis
Judge: John Hawkes

1972
The Burning and Other Stories,
Jack Cady
Judge: Joyce Carol Oates

1971
*Old Morals, Small Continents,
Darker Times,*
Philip F. O'Connor
Judge: George P. Elliott

1970
The Beach Umbrella,
Cyrus Colter
Judges: Vance Bourjaily
and Kurt Vonnegut, Jr.